Anybody Want to Play
WAR?

Anybody Want to Play WAR?

Tommy B. Smith

Seventh

StarShadow

Cover art and design: Olivia Pro Design

Cover art in this book copyright © 2019 Olivia Pro Design & Seventh Star Press, LLC.

Editor: Stephen Zimmer

Published by Seventh Star Press, LLC.

ISBN Number: 978-1-948042-84-0

Seventh Star Press

www.seventhstarpress.com

info@seventhstarpress.com

Publisher's Note:

Anybody Want to Play WAR? is a work of fiction. All names, characters, and places are the product of the author's imagination, used in fictitious manner. Any resemblances to actual persons, places, locales, events, etc. are purely coincidental.

Printed in the United States of America

First Edition

In memory of Christopher Daniel Morphis

1980

Day of the Dog

Sunlight blinked between the clouds one fair Saturday afternoon as a yellow-eyed hound tore a man's throat out behind a gas station.

A woman with a mane of dark, fluffy hair, walking along the broken sidewalk with her eight-year-old child, saw the dog charging up the street. When the sight of the creature's bloody muzzle registered, she hastened from the street and yanked her child away with her.

An elderly man now stood in the dog's path. He too saw the blood in its fur and teeth, as well as the keen savagery in its strange yellow eyes. He scrambled for the imagined safety of a nearby home.

Instead of pursuing, the dog's brown head turned. Its eyes locked on another individual at the side of the street, a teenager. Their eyes held.

For several seconds, Bryce Gallo stared back at the dog until it shot toward him and lunged.

It drove him to the street on his back. With a flurry of

spittle, its teeth latched into his face, digging in deep. The beast fought to rip the flesh away.

Bryce's senses spun. He struggled for survival, pummeling the dog with his arms, pushing against the daze consuming him. Grinding its teeth in, the hound wrenched its head back.

Bryce's flesh tore. He gasped. Blood, tears, and canine saliva leaked down his face.

It required a true effort of will to cram his hand into his right pocket, withdraw the pocketknife, and unfold its four-and-a-half inch stainless steel blade. Desperate, he stabbed it deep into the dog's rage-quivering neck.

The dog reeled, grunted, and squealed. Its jaws slipped free. The canine staggered aside and darted across the street.

With a screech of brakes and a blasting horn, a white Cadillac struck the dog and smeared it across the street in a mess of red, white, and brown.

The hound's death broke the fog of fear stalling everyone around. A woman screamed. Her boy stood transfixed.

A diminutive older man shouted, "Call an ambulance!"

Bryce pressed his hands against his bleeding face. It hurt, it burned, and that was his base assessment of the pain through his shock. Blood seeped between his fingers. He couldn't restrain a choked cry. Wild dizziness consumed him.

The hard street, the blood, and the pain fell away in another instant, swallowed by minutes and hours of incomprehension.

Bryce lay in a white hospital bed. Bandages wrapped his face. He tried to speak, but it came out garbled. Medications coursed through his bloodstream, rendering him woozy and lightheaded.

"Bryce? Can you hear me?"

He wasn't sure who had spoken. A nurse in white with short, blond hair stood at his bedside. Some distance past her stood his mother and stepfather.

For his initial waking moments, his mother approached and remained close, murmuring faint reassurances in the aftermath of the dog's assault.

It had followed him into his dreams. Over and over, he fought for his life against it, but the dog kept winning and no one would do a thing to help him.

His mother pleaded with the nurses and the doctor until Richard said, "Elaine, please."

Crossing her arms, she fell into a quiet huff. When her eyes returned to her son on the hospital bed, her irritation melted into concern. Bryce could see it on her face, but she said little. She just kept looking at him.

It didn't get much better when the bandages came away, when the medical bill arrived, or when the stitches were out. Bryce had fought for his life and won, but not without cost. A stark red scar ran beneath his left eye and down to the bottom of his jaw.

The Detour

I

Every time he looked into the mirror, Bryce saw the fresh scar twisting down the side of his face. Others would see it as they passed. Everyone would stare as those bystanders had when he fought for everything against that crazed dog.

People would ask questions. They would ask him why he looked the way he did, what was wrong with his face, whether it hurt, and an assortment of other questions.

Bryce didn't care to confront the hundred stares or the thousand questions, but he was due back for classes today, and that was all he could think about. He hadn't slept much.

After a warm shower, he ran a comb through his wet, dark-brown hair. He skipped looking in the mirror this time and revisited his room to snatch his navy-blue jacket from the closet. He threw it around his shoulders and sat on the rumpled red-and-blue comforter of the bed until his mother came to his door.

She leaned in. Her curly brown hair fountained down around her head like she had stabbed a fork into a light socket. "Bryce. Don't be late."

Agitated, he raised his head, wondering why she was bothering him when he still had more than enough time. She stared at him, as if waiting for some form of an answer.

"Fine," Bryce said. He stood, walked to the door, opened it wider, and walked past her into the hallway.

"Why are you taking your jacket?" his mother asked, following him. "It isn't cold outside."

"Just in case," he said, and headed toward the door.

"Don't you want a bowl of cereal?" she asked.

"I don't want to be late, do I?"

"But it's early."

"Then I'll be early."

He stepped outside. He expected her to follow him out but heard nothing else from his mother as he crossed the bumpy front yard to the road.

Under a dim, cloudy sky, he turned left, following the road. Bryce felt better wearing his jacket today, even if it wasn't cold outside. It made him a bit more comfortable, as did the folded knife in his pocket.

After what happened with the dog, he didn't think he would ever leave his pocketknife behind again. Without it, he might be dead.

At its end, this road met Dartmoor. The bus would stop at the corner. He was early, and none of the other kids were there. Good. He didn't feel like encountering any of them today, especially Nate, the annoying skinny kid with the blond bowl-cut and gapped front teeth who always walked around with an idiotic smirk on his face.

A different road branched to his right. This one curved back to the left to intersect with Dartmoor at another point. Bryce glanced around to verify the road was clear, crossed the street, and took the other road instead.

"So, I got a little lost," he murmured to himself. "Missed the bus today. Oh, well."

He rounded the curve to approach Dartmoor, a busier street with traffic speeding by in both directions. When Bryce found an opening, he ran across. On the other side, he slowed and proceeded down the next adjoining street into another neighborhood.

At the end of one driveway, a large man with tufts of graying hair circling the top of his otherwise bald head hunched in front of a black mailbox. With a handful of mail, he lifted his eyes toward Bryce. To Bryce's discomfort, the man watched for some time, but when Bryce neared, the resident closed his mailbox and ambled back to the front door of his house.

Bryce passed the house and continued along the squiggly suburban road. Once he had the opportunity, he turned onto another road. This road, bordered on each side by houses mostly brown and maroon, continued for a while.

Violent barking upended Bryce's heart into machine-gun panic. A white German shepherd charged across a dying lawn at him. Bryce jammed a hand into his pocket for his pocketknife.

The dog's chain snapped taut. Straining, the canine barked and lunged against the chain.

Bryce took a slow breath and fumbled to escape the monster tension that had seized him. His heart hammered.

He forced his steps away from the chained dog but watched it as he walked. Even down the street with the dog out of sight, he still heard it barking and kept his hand on his pocketknife.

II

In the middle of west downtown suburbia, the white facade of Bryce's house was a painted-over image of pristine contradiction. They had moved into the place shortly after his mother had married Richard, but Bryce remembered another home and a time when things were different.

It had been Bryce and his mother in those days in the old neighborhood, along with his Uncle Jax. Uncle Jax had been out and around, seen some things, knew a few things. He had seen war.

One night, vandals shattered one of their bedroom windows and threw Bryce's mother into a panic. She had called the police, but they were late to arrive and never found anyone on the premises.

She was afraid the vandals would come back. She mentioned it to Jax in a hushed voice.

"I'll look forward to it," he replied over his glass of Jim Beam on ice. "The way I see it, if you're going to start something, you'd better be ready to finish it or else somebody else is going to finish it for you."

When he looked over and noticed Bryce standing there, he added, "Am I right, buddy?"

Jax tossed back the last trace of whiskey in his glass. Visibly uncomfortable, Bryce's mother said to her son, "Honey, why don't you go on to bed? It's late."

Meanwhile, Uncle Jax helped himself to another glass of whiskey. Bryce remembered his mother hadn't liked Jax's heavy drinking, but there were worse things—at least until cirrhosis of the liver got him.

The memories of his earlier youth trailed to the back of Bryce's mind as his attention fell onto houses of peeling paint and frames in disrepair. Trash littered a few front lawns. Dirty diapers decorated the lawn of one splotchy brown house with a plastic-sheeting window.

Another dog, a Doberman, barked from the front of a fenced-in property. Bryce tensed again. He wondered if the dog could leap over the fence. He returned his hand to the pocket where his knife rested.

Keeping the dog in his clear sight, he considered cutting back through an unfenced property. He could reach Hatch Street by that route.

When he made the attempt, a man with a patch of gray hair on his bumpy head confronted him from a green stool at the side of the property's carport. He wore an ugly gray-and-green-striped collared shirt and an even uglier sneer.

"What are you doing here?" the man asked.

Anybody Want to Play WAR?

"Trying to get up to Hatch Street," Bryce said. "I thought this way would be faster."

"Go around," the man said. "And don't ever set foot on my property again."

Annoyed, Bryce returned to the road and continued his walk.

"What a jackass," he muttered.

When he came to the next four-way stop, he took a left and directed his course toward Hatch Street. The buzzing traffic here made him nervous. He hoped his mother or Richard, or anyone else he knew, wouldn't see him out here walking when he was supposed to be at school.

Cars and trucks shot by on the busy street. Bryce kept his head down as he walked. Ahead, on his right, he saw Tuck's Corner Store.

He had a few dollars in his pocket and decided to stop in. When he opened the store's glass front door, a bell jingled.

The clerk looked up from a newspaper when Bryce entered, and watched him as he walked between rows of snacks and confections to the back cooler, where he picked out a cold bottle of orange soda.

Bryce returned to the counter, met the clerk's gaze, and laid down a dollar. With an abrupt cha-*ching,* the clerk pulled the change from the register and slid it onto the counter. Bryce took his change without speaking, pocketed it, and left.

Instead of proceeding back to the street, he circled the store to the small back parking lot where only a worn white sedan was parked. He sat down at the back edge of the lot. With his pocketknife, he pried the cap from his soda. Tossing the cap aside, he took a deep drink of cold, fizzy orange refreshment.

He hadn't managed to face school today. So what? So as long as no one knew, it wouldn't be a problem. His goal for the day, he decided, was to make sure his mother and Richard never found out about this little detour.

The worst part of it still nagged him, however. No matter

how long he tried to avoid the future, it was coming, and he couldn't stop it. Horrible days loomed head.

The store's back door creaked open. The clerk stepped out with his hands on his hips. "What are you doing back here?" he demanded.

"Drinking my drink," Bryce answered.

"You got no business being back here. Beat it."

Bryce stood up and started away again. For an instant, he considered turning around and throwing his bottle of orange soda at the man, hopefully hitting him in the face, but he didn't need anybody calling the cops on him today.

He did stop to look back at the store clerk. The man glared at him. After a moment's deliberation, Bryce resumed walking.

III

Bryce held his footsteps along the shoulder of Hatch Street. The traffic kept zipping by, but over the next hour, it lessened. His thoughts wandered to other concerns, such as tomorrow.

The others at school had already heard about him, he guessed. They knew about the dog attacking him.

He imagined himself hurrying down the crowded school hall with his head down, grabbing his books from his locker as fast as he could. When he stepped into his first class of the day, Mrs. Davenport's class, she would address him. Everyone would turn their heads toward him. Some of them would whisper.

Bryce already hated school, and things would only get worse from here. The days ahead would feel like months. Looking toward the future was like staring at a dead-end wall.

The road to nowhere stretched on.

He lifted the soda for another drink. It had lost its refreshing chill, but he had paid for it, so he kept drinking. With another chug, he finished it off and almost tossed the empty bottle off to the side. The coming police cruiser changed his mind.

He hoped he hadn't been too conspicuous in his sudden, startled movement. He tried to relax and act naturally but had a feeling he was doing a horrible job of it.

The cops might stop to question him or even haul him in for truancy. Bryce stared at his shoes. He gripped the glass bottle in his right hand and didn't stop walking. The police car slowed down, driving beside him.

He was busted, he realized.

Then, to his surprise, the police vehicle accelerated on. He released the breath he had been holding but didn't look up. The police car departed with the rest of the traffic along Hatch Street, and only after it was long gone did Bryce lift his head again.

Farther along, he passed an old boarded-up, closed-down furniture store on the left side of the street. Past it, more accessible on his right, was a narrow wooden building divided into two shops with separate entrances, a gift shop and a florist. A round brown trash can stood outside, between the two doors. Bryce took advantage of it to get rid of the empty bottle.

Well past the little shops, a dingy gray apartment building stood to the right. Tired of the busy traffic, Bryce left the roadside to cross the parking lot and cut behind the apartments.

A few metal trash cans sat at the far end of the apartments' back lot. An old olive-green couch rested near the trash cans. Two people stood near the couch, a thin black man with big hair and a beard, wearing baggy pants and a white tank top, and a dark-featured woman with billowy, blue-and-green clothing and turquoise hoop earrings.

Seeing Bryce, both turned. The man motioned him over.

"Can you come over here and help me out for a minute?" he called.

"With what?" Bryce asked.

"Just for a minute, that's it. Help me move this couch

over?"

"Okay," Bryce said. "Sure."

When Bryce came over, the woman moved out of their way and the man moved to take the other end of the couch. Together, Bryce and the other man hoisted it away from the trash cans.

"That'll do it," the man said. He lowered his end of the couch.

Bryce set his end down. The man in the white tank top came around to sit down on the couch.

"All right, thanks," he said.

Bryce started to walk away, but the man spoke again.

"You in a hurry to be somewhere?" he asked.

"Not really," Bryce said, "but I don't have any reason to hang around here."

"Fair enough," the man said. "Thanks for helping me out with the couch, little man."

The man's tone was friendly enough, although being called "little man" kind of annoyed Bryce.

"It's Bryce."

"Thanks for the help, Mister Bryce. My name's Jones, but everybody calls me Wheels." He extended his hand.

Bryce felt awkward about walking off now. He came over and shook the man's hand.

"This is Paloma," Wheels said, introducing the woman who accompanied him. Paloma nodded, but didn't approach, so Bryce just nodded back.

"So, we're not total strangers anymore," Wheels said. "And if you're not in a hurry to be anywhere, why don't you hang around with us for a little while? We got nowhere to be in a big hurry, either."

Wheels

I

Wheels didn't seem to notice the scar, hadn't brought it up, and hadn't appeared to look twice at it. Maybe that was why Bryce came back. He felt he could lower his guard an inch and talk to the man who reclined on one end of the green couch.

The woman, Paloma, still stood nearby, but she remained quiet.

Wheels leaned back and motioned toward the other end of the couch.

"Plenty of room over there," he said to Bryce. "Feel free."

"No thanks," Bryce said. "That couch looks dirty. I don't want to get shit all over my clothes."

"It's not dirty," Wheels said. "Just old, that's all."

"Why did you want to move it over here?" Bryce asked.

"Because I don't want to sit by that nasty-smelling trash."

"I guess that makes sense."

"Where you from, Bryce?"

"I live over on the west end. You?"

"I live right here."

"In the parking lot?"

"Shit, no. That's my apartment over there. Paloma lives in the one downstairs from me. What, did you think we were

13

sleeping out here by the trash every night?"

"I didn't think anything. I was just asking."

As Wheels regarded Bryce, he reached down to take a pack of cigarettes and matchbook from his faded jeans pocket. Striking a light, he lit up his cigarette.

He took a deep puff, let it out, and put the rest of his cigarettes away along with the matches. "You're from the west side, huh?" Wheels asked.

"We've been over there for a few years now. I'm not from there."

"Oh? Where you from then?"

Bryce waved his hand east in an "over in that general direction" gesture. Wheels responded with a thoughtful nod. He took another slow puff of his cigarette and blew out a stream of smoke.

"Probably good for you that you moved," Wheels said. "Not always so safe over that way anymore." He paused to watch the cigarette smoke drifting upward. "How old are you, if you don't mind me asking?"

"Eighteen," Bryce lied. He abruptly noticed Paloma's dark eyes watching him from the corner of his vision.

"Eighteen," Wheels echoed. "You out of high school?"

"Yeah." It was another nonchalant lie. He noticed Paloma still watching him. Her steady gaze began to make him uncomfortable.

"Want a smoke?" Wheels offered Bryce. He shifted back against the couch and crossed one tattered sneaker over the other.

"Yeah, I'll take one," Bryce said. Wheels went for his pack of cigarettes again, slid one out, and passed it over.

Bryce placed the cigarette between his lips. Wheels struck another match and gave him a light. Bryce nodded and took a smoke.

With a single cough, he removed the cigarette from his mouth, hesitated, then took a slower drag.

Bryce didn't call himself a smoker, the same way Patrick

Anybody Want to Play WAR?

Finn didn't, but that didn't mean Bryce and Finn wouldn't take a cigarette whenever they could get one.

"Let's start up a little support group, what do you say?" Finn said to him one day as they smoked a couple of cigarettes Finn had stolen from his dad. They smoked behind the school library building and watched for any approaching teachers or whiny tattletale students.

"A group?" Bryce had replied. "What, for smokers?"

"I was thinking more for people who got better shit to do than this," Finn said. *The School Haters' Club*. How's that sound?"

"And then what?"

"We all skip school, man. What else?"

When the bell went off, both boys snubbed their cigarettes on the brick wall of the library building. Then it became a rush to their lockers for their books and to class, chewing gum along the frantic course to hide their cigarette breath.

"I've been doing maintenance out here for a little while," Wheels said, retrieving Bryce's attention and glancing over at Paloma. "Almost six months now, right? After the quake hit, the place needed a lot of work. I have some skills, and I made this little agreement when I came in here. I'm kind of a jack-of-all-trades."

Paloma, as usual so far, had nothing to add. Wheels and Bryce continued smoking in what became a contemplative silence.

Not many people talked about the quake anymore, although it had only happened the year before. It seemed strange, trying to ignore a wound that was so fresh.

Wheels was an exception, the sort of man who could look at you and acknowledge, "Yeah, that happened."

Of everything Bryce recalled from that day, between the bathroom mirror's rattling and his mother's figurines trembling up on the bookshelf, he most remembered spending the rest of the day in the living room, in front of the television. His mother had been stressed, Richard grimly silent, and Bryce eating a snapping, crackling, popping bowl of Rice Krispies while the three of them watched news of the destruction and the River Bridge's collapse.

Though the construction crews were dedicated and determined throughout the course of the subsequent rebuilding project, some people would never feel comfortable driving over that bridge again.

"So, why do you call yourself Wheels?" Bryce asked, lowering his cigarette-hand to his side.

"I didn't come up with that," Wheels said. "Other people did. You know what's funny? I can't even drive. Not legally. I used to work down at the Spring Market, and one night I went to this get-together, you see. Lots of drinking, throwing around some dice, you know. Next thing I know, I'm waking up on somebody's couch and the whole room's spinning. By the time I got it together, I saw the clock and it was noon and I knew I was supposed to be at work at eight in the morning. I jumped up and got in a big hurry. I ran outside, got in my car, took off like crazy to get to work, thinking I was four hours late. I turned into the parking lot there at the Spring Market and a car backed up all of a sudden, right in front of me. I swerved around it and ran right up on the storefront. Hit it. It was made out of glass, too, so I shattered the whole damned front of the store. Yeah, that was my last day working there. Lost my driver's license, too. You know what the funniest thing is? It was twelve-something past midnight, not twelve noon. I was so out of it, I didn't notice, even with it being dark outside. But yeah, that's when everybody started calling me *Wheels.*"

II

Bryce finished his cigarette and went to throw it in the trash. When he lifted the trash can lid, Wheels spoke up.

"Watch out, little man—sorry, Bryce—make sure you put

that thing out. We don't need any trash fires around here."

Bryce extinguished it against the side of the trash can. "That good enough?"

"That's better. Go ahead."

Bryce dropped the cigarette butt into the trash and replaced the round metal lid. A gust of wind came through and ruffled Bryce's hair. He reached up to straighten it back and pulled his jacket more securely around him.

"I better get up there and finish what I started," Wheels said. He stood from the couch.

"I've been clearing out #4," he elaborated. "Some married couple with lots of, uh, problems. Seems the man's wife and girlfriend met and didn't get along too much. They got out of here and never came back. You need a couch?" He patted the side of the couch. "Not new, but it looks like nobody's coming back for it, so finders, keepers."

"No thanks," Bryce said.

"I'll get it hauled out of here." Wheels dusted off his jeans and took a step toward the apartment building but caught himself, and turned back around.

"Thanks for the help," he said. "Take it easy."

"Thanks for the cigarette," Bryce said.

"Good to meet you," Paloma said, startling Bryce. He couldn't think of a response, simple as it should be, but it didn't matter much because both of them were already walking away.

Games

Bryce walked beside a chain mesh fence paralleling Hatch Street. The traffic continued shooting past, but he kept his eyes to the ground and his hands in his pockets. He felt the reassuring stainless steel of his pocketknife, and his thoughts wandered back to that old house from his earlier childhood.

In particular, he thought of the day Uncle Jax called him over and said, "I got something for you."

When he held out his hands, Uncle Jax gave him the pocketknife.

"It's a Sterling. It's yours now."

Uncle Jax could have offered to show him, but instead he sat back and let Bryce work it out on his own. Once the blade was out, it locked into place with a click. When Bryce tried to close it and couldn't, Uncle Jax reached for his glass of whiskey.

"How do you do it?" Bryce asked. After a sip of whiskey, Uncle Jax set his glass down, leaned over to take the knife, pushed in a section of the handle, and folded the blade shut.

"And that's how you do it," Uncle Jax said.

When Bryce turned to leave, his uncle spoke up again.

"What do you say?"

"What? Oh. Thank you."

"You're welcome. Now be careful with that. It isn't a toy. It's sharp."

When his mother saw the pocketknife, her eyes narrowed, but she didn't say anything to Bryce. She did ask Uncle Jax about it.

"What if he cuts himself?"

"He won't," Uncle Jax said.

"But what if he does?"

"You're his mother," he replied. "If he does something like that, I'm sure you'll take it away from him."

She didn't like his response, but she let it be.

Bryce was always careful with his pocketknife. He respected its sharp, steel blade.

He remembered carving that blade into the soft gray bark of the big tree behind their old house, first making a careful *B*, then a sloppy, angular *G*. He wondered if his initials were still there. He hadn't seen that place in years. They never drove through that area anymore.

Murders and theft had escalated over there since, Bryce had heard, especially over the past year. There were a few unexplained disappearances. Bryce, along with his mother, Richard, and countless others who had seen them on the news and in the newspaper, supposed the victims were most likely dead.

From earlier this year, Bryce remembered catching a televised news segment about a murder behind one of the motels in east downtown. While cleaning the alley behind the motel, the motel's manager was stabbed multiple times and robbed of his cigarettes, the six dollars in his wallet, and the brown-bagged tuna sandwich he had brought for lunch that day.

Not always so safe over that way anymore, Wheels had said, and he was right. But at least Bryce was only watching it on the news instead of living in the middle of it, even if he didn't care much for his current neighborhood.

Anybody Want to Play WAR?

Of course, there had been the one strange incident over on the west end, one of those which hadn't officially been labeled as a murder but as a disappearance, although it was said blood marked the house's interior.

Then, that crazed yellow-eyed dog came along and killed the owner of a gas station before it got to Bryce. If Bryce hadn't had his pocketknife, he would surely be dead.

Amid the gruesome speculations, Bryce wondered what time it was. He had been roaming for at least a couple of hours.

He saw a Laundromat ahead on the right. Once closer, he decided to stop in and check the time.

As soon as he stepped inside, a heavy body collided into him, a heavyset sixties-ish woman in a red-spotted white outfit. She carried a basket of laundry under one arm. The woman grunted something unintelligible and pushed past him for the door.

He looked between the few customers who sorted laundry or waited for their spinning clothing and linens to finish. An *Asteroids* arcade game stood against the wall in one corner. He spotted a service window in another corner. Where was the clock around here?

He approached the open orange-lined window and its protruding counter. He leaned against the counter and peered into the area past it, where an old woman with gray curly hair rummaged through a cardboard box full of what appeared to be smaller boxes of powdered soap. Eventually, she glanced back to see Bryce at the window.

She came over with one of the powdered soap boxes and thumped it on the counter.

"Did you need something?" she asked.

"Do you know what time it is?" Bryce asked.

"You'll have to look at the clock."

"I couldn't find a clock."

She leaned over the counter. Bryce stepped back.

"Any of you know what time it is?" the woman called.

A woman with curly silver hair, sitting on a bench and reading a magazine, checked her watch. "Almost 10:45," she said, and went back to her magazine.

School didn't let out until 3:00 p.m.

"Anything else?" the laundry desk woman asked Bryce.

"Do you have change?"

"Yeah," she said. Bryce pulled out a couple of dollars and handed them through the window.

The woman took his money and reached into some unseen source beneath her counter, digging through the change there and counting out eight quarters. She placed them in a stack on the counter.

Bryce took his quarters, pocketed most of them, and went to play *Asteroids*. He had hours. There were worse ways to pass the time than destroying space junk. He stuck in a quarter and started a game.

He spun his ship and tapped the button, firing into the asteroids. With a follow-up flurry of shots, he eradicated most of the smaller oncoming pieces.

As he cleared the screen and his score climbed, an odd self-consciousness pestered him. He could almost feel eyes on him. When he looked away from the game, he saw a little boy with close-cut light-blond hair and freckly features standing there in an oversized white tee-shirt.

The boy belonged to the frumpy woman, who busied herself with stuffing laundry into one of the washers. What the hell did the kid want? Bryce realized the boy was staring at the ugly red scar on his face. The close scrutiny made him uncomfortable.

On the screen, asteroids overtook his ship with a crash.

Bryce turned his back to the kid and returned to his game. He had lives left and didn't want to waste a quarter.

It became harder to focus. He sped his ship away from a group of asteroids, firing along the route. He struck more than one, but the array of fast-moving pieces crashed into him.

Anybody Want to Play WAR?

He stood for a moment with his hands on the arcade game's controls. He felt an anger simmering.

He glanced back to see if the kid was still staring, but he had gone back to his mother. Bryce turned back to the game and launched into blasting everything in sight.

II

With a crash, another life ended, and it was game over.

Bryce reached into his pocket for another quarter but considered he had been playing for some time now. He jingled the remaining quarters in his pocket. After a minute, he decided to head for the door. He didn't want to be late getting back, for sure.

The traffic had thickened along Hatch Street. Bryce guessed it was around the lunch hour, noon, or sometime after. He remained along Hatch Street until he neared Tuck's store again, where he made another stop.

The clerk didn't pay any attention to him this time. Bryce scanned the store's interior until he found a circular clock on the wall behind the clerk.

It was barely past 1:00. He had plenty of time and would take it slow on the rest of the walk back. Getting home too early would be worse than arriving late. He tossed around lies and made-up scenarios in his mind in case his mother asked him about his day at school. He needed to be prepared.

From the corner of his eye, Bryce saw the clerk watching him now. He turned toward the man, who looked away at the same second.

Bryce chuckled beneath his breath. The man could stare, but he wouldn't say shit, would he?

He went back to pick out a can of soda, a cheap, generic cola this time, and he threw in a small snack-pack of cheese and crackers since he hadn't eaten anything today. The clerk rang up his purchase, muttering his total. Bryce paid, scooped up his snack and can of cola, and left.

Continuing back, he munched on the crackers and cheese. When he made a left turn back to the neighborhood streets he had traveled before, he popped open the soda. It hissed and fizzed. He stopped by the road, put the cool can to his lips, and took a deep drink.

He resumed walking, and in another three drinks, finished the soda. Tossing the can to the roadside, he kicked it up the road.

A loud barking surprised him. Muscles tense and fists clenched, he almost went for his knife, but he saw the dog secured behind a fence. He recognized the Doberman from before. He sighed, forced himself to relax, and gave the can another kick. It bounced onto a green lawn.

He moved to kick it back onto the street when a voice shouted, "Hey!"

It was the disgruntled man from earlier, the one who had told him not to set foot on his property again. He sat outside his front door on his same green stool. He glared at Bryce with his bulging bug-eyes.

"Don't you kick that trash down my street!" he spat. "You pick it up!"

Keeping eye contact with the man, Bryce kicked the can again. He waited for the man's eyes to pop right out of his head. He had a brief mental image of kicking a couple of eyeballs along the road.

The man sat there and gaped. Bryce kept kicking that can all the way up the street.

Questions

I

When Bryce reached Evelyn Drive via his roundabout route, he saw his mother's white Pontiac in the driveway. Richard's black Buick was absent. He wouldn't be home until after five.

Bryce did his best to time his return at around fifteen minutes past three, give or take a few minutes. He couldn't be completely sure of the time without a watch. He guessed he was early.

Since he could see the bus stop from here, he decided he would watch for it, and once it appeared, he would go on inside with no questions asked. At least that's how he hoped it would go. He sat on the concrete of the carport to the right side of the Pontiac and looked toward the end of the street.

The front door of the neighboring house opened. A short woman with fluffy brown hair stepped outside—Rhonda, their neighbor. Her husband, a truck driver from what Bryce understood, was seldom home. Rhonda sometimes talked to Bryce's mother, usually about the most boring topics imaginable.

Now Rhonda looked straight at Bryce. She jerked her head away the moment she realized eye contact.

She walked to her mailbox, opened it, and removed a

few envelopes. While she sifted through her mail at the end of her driveway, Bryce stood up. She had already seen him anyway.

About this time, the big orange side of the school bus caught Bryce's vision. It stopped at the corner. A few figures climbed out.

Bryce walked to the front door of his house, unlocked it, opened it, and stepped inside.

The polished round wooden kitchen table held a clutter of bills. One of the table's chairs had been pulled out. A set of car keys were splayed on top of the stack of bills.

Bryce moved for the hallway, toward his bedroom. He made an effort to keep his steps soft, but when he stepped into the hall, the floor creaked.

"Bryce?" his mother's voice called from the living room.

"What?" he answered.

"You're back early?"

"Early? It's past three."

"Is it? Oh. How was school?"

"Great. Just great."

She gave no further reply. Bryce went to his room. He stepped over to the cedar dresser against the right-hand wall. A radio rested on top of the dresser. He switched it on. Once he found a passable station, he sat on the edge of his bed.

He considered grabbing a magazine from his hidden stash but guessed his mother would be in to check on him soon, so he laid against his flat pillow and listened to the garbage on the radio. It played old stuff from the 50s. Right now, it annoyed him, but he didn't feel like getting up to change it.

His eyes fell to a poster on his wall, an angry rhinoceros. He had gone through some other posters, but his mother had taken each of them down. She hadn't said anything about it, but when he came home, they were missing. He knew she had taken them down. She didn't like him looking at pretty girls, apparently, but taking away a couple of posters wasn't going to stop that.

Anybody Want to Play WAR?

There were plenty of girls at school, although Bryce never saw them with their legs spread apart like the steaming-hot brunette on one of his vanished posters. The girls at school were nice to look at it, but that was about it.

In general, he didn't like most of the other people at school, and he liked them even less now that he had to face them all with his face marked by the awful scar. He knew they would swoop in on him like a bunch of vultures.

Finn bummed him cigarettes, though, which helped to calm his anxiety. Bryce could stand Finn for short periods of time. Between the two of them, they were just trying to survive high school.

Bryce's thoughts drifted back to girls. He daydreamed about that girl who sat near him in Mrs. Davenport's class, Brittany, with her deep-auburn hair, milky skin, and firm bosom.

He edged toward the ventilation shaft in the corner floor. Lifting the vent, he reached in to feel around for the hidden magazines.

The phone rang. An internal warning spurred Bryce to withdraw and replace the vent cover. After a single ring, the phone stopped. His mother had answered it, and now her footsteps were coming down the hallway toward his door.

Bryce stood up to turn down the radio's volume. A moment later, his mother opened his door. Her hair was tamer than this morning. She appeared less like a trapped animal.

"Phone," she said. "It's for you."

Bryce picked up his ugly green phone. "Hello?"

"Hey, Bryce, man, where were you today?" It was Finn.

Bryce looked over at his mother. She withdrew and shut the door.

"Watch what you say," Bryce said into the phone. "My mom might listen in."

"You mean you decided to skip and didn't tell me?"

"What did I just say, Finn?"

"Sorry. Everybody at school heard about the dog, but you probably already know that. They're saying it really tore you up."

"They heard right. But yeah, that's the thing—"

"Hello?"

"Mom, I got it," Bryce said, agitated.

"Okay," his mother said. "I'll hang up now."

Click.

"What's going on?" Finn asked. "You coming to school tomorrow?"

"I don't know," Bryce said.

"What, you dropping out?"

"I need some time, more time than the doctors gave me."

"But you're gonna come back, right?"

"I guess I have to."

"How's it look?"

"Horrible."

"That bad?"

"Yeah."

"Can I come over?"

Bryce almost muttered a dismissal. *Hell no, I'm too tired, too miserable, my mom's acting crazy*—which wasn't true today, not yet anyway, but it was an excuse.

Instead, Bryce reconsidered and said with some hesitation, "Hold on a minute." He opened his bedroom door. "Mom?"

"What is it?" she replied from the kitchen.

"Can Finn come over?"

"No. We need to have a talk later."

"About what?"

"Just tell him he can't come over today."

"Why?"

"You heard me."

Bryce closed his bedroom door and returned to the phone.

Anybody Want to Play WAR?

"Something's weird. My mom's saying you can't come over."

"Oh, really?" Finn replied.

"I'm thinking she found out I skipped or something."

"Good luck with that one. Ciao."

II

Bryce had liked the idea of Finn coming over. Because no one at school had seen the damage to his face, letting Finn see it first felt like an easier slide into that inevitability.

But instead, he would be stuck with only his mother and Richard tonight, and his mother wanted to have a talk. He didn't like the kind of talks he expected this one might be. He had a feeling he would be listening to a bunch of bullshit.

Sure, I'll do this and that, and yes ma'am, yes sir, I won't do whatever it is anymore. Only Bryce wouldn't say any of that. He would sit there watching the bubbles in his glass of cola, letting the babble flow into one ear and out the other until he could go back to his room and shut himself in.

That time wasn't far away. His mother's footsteps approached his door again.

"Bryce," she said from outside. "You need to come to the dinner table."

He came to the table, pulled out a chair, and sat down. His mother milled around in the kitchen. She came back to place a large, white ceramic bowl of pot roast, potatoes, and carrots on the table. Next, she brought over a cloth-covered plate of rolls. She took the chair to Bryce's right. Richard came last and filled the chair directly across from Bryce.

They made their plates and, for a while, ate in silence. Bryce took his time. He wasn't that hungry and wanted to get this over with. Richard glanced up from his plate every so often. He reached up to brush his gray mustache but went back to his meal without comment.

Finally, Bryce's mother laid her fork on her plate with a

gentle clink and asked, "Bryce, do you want to tell me why you smelled like cigarette smoke today?"

"Why beat around the bush, Elaine?" Richard said. "We know why. He was smoking." He didn't look up from his roast and potatoes.

"I want an answer from *him*." Elaine's eyes were cold.

"I didn't smell like cigarettes," Bryce said.

"That's a lie and you know it." Anger squeezed his mother's voice. "I smelled it earlier. I can smell cigarette smoke a mile away."

"That's some useful talent," Bryce said. "Maybe you smelled somebody else's cigarette smoke a mile down the road."

Richard put down his fork and pointed his gaze at Bryce. "Your mother asked you a question. You need to give her an honest answer."

"That's one opinion," Bryce said.

"It's a fact," Richard said, "and I'll tell you something else. Your mother and I don't appreciate your disrespect around here. You need to get something straight. We're the adults here, and while we're paying the bills and you're living under this roof, you'll respect your mother and you *will* follow the rules of this house."

Bryce pushed his plate away. "I'm done. Thanks for dinner, mom. I'm going back to my room."

"No, you aren't," Richard said. "You're going to stay right here. If you're out sneaking cigarettes, that's a crime, do you realize that? If the police catch you, who do you think is going to get you out of jail?"

"Nobody, probably," Bryce said.

"Because it'll be your own fault," Richard said. "And to be honest, I think it might do you some good to sit in jail for a day or two."

"Richard," Elaine whispered. Her anger hadn't subsided, but some part of her thought her husband had gone a touch too far.

Anybody Want to Play WAR?

"We haven't even gotten to the center of the issue here, Elaine," Richard said. "Why don't you ask him why he wasn't at school today?"

"Who says I wasn't at school?" Bryce asked.

His mother didn't reply. She clenched her hands together in her lap and looked down.

They knew he was lying, that much was clear. They had already been talking, formulating their plan of attack.

"I got a phone call," Elaine said. "They said you were out walking down Hatch Street this morning."

"They? Who?"

"It doesn't matter."

"You know what?" Bryce said. "You're right. I skipped school today. You want to know why? Look at me."

Richard and Elaine exchanged a glance.

"I don't buy it," Richard said. "You've had time to recover. You knew you had to go back to school today. It's no excuse. I don't always like my job, but I do it anyway. I deal with my problems because I'm a man, and you'll have to be a man too someday, so it's time you started learning how to act like one."

"If that means acting like you, then no, I don't think that'll ever happen," Bryce said.

Richard threw down his napkin and stood up. "I'm tired of your disrespectful attitude. Things are going to change. Your mother and I will see to that. There won't be any more excuses out of you, and I'd better not hear another lie out of your mouth again. Tomorrow morning, I'm taking you to school."

"You don't have to do that," Elaine said, her voice quiet. "I can take him. You have to work."

"No, I'll take him," Richard said. "You've put up with enough out of him lately. I'll deal with it."

Elaine sank into her chair. Bryce stared at his plate. "Are we done now?" he asked.

"I've said what I have to say," Richard said. He returned

to his seat, picked up his fork, and resumed eating.

Bryce left his chair for the hallway. "Don't you want to finish your dinner?" his mother called after him.

"I'm finished," Bryce said. He stepped into his room, closed the door, turned on the radio, and tossed himself onto the bed.

Anxiety High

I

Bryce woke up several times during the night. When the earliest morning light signified the dreaded day's approach, sleep abandoned him altogether.

His mother cracked open the bedroom door. "Bryce? You need to get up. Don't be late."

He dragged himself out of bed, tired, and took a steaming shower. Afterward, he combed his hair and threw on some jeans and a maroon short-sleeved shirt.

Stepping into this day already felt like dragging his feet across broken glass. It didn't help when he saw Richard already sitting at the kitchen table, dressed and ready. A cup of black coffee sat in front of him. He held the day's newspaper propped against the table's edge. He looked up when Bryce walked in, lifted his cup of coffee for a sip, careful to avoid wetting his moustache, and went back to the paper.

Bryce took a box of Rice Krispies from the top of the refrigerator and poured a bowl. He sloshed milk into it and ate his breakfast standing up. Once finished, he dropped the bowl into the sink and plucked a can of soda out of the refrigerator.

"Are you sure you should be drinking that stuff first thing

in the morning?" his mother asked, having stepped from the living room into the kitchen.

"Just hurry up," Richard said. He inspected his watch. "We'll be leaving soon."

Bryce guzzled his soda. When Richard folded the paper under his arm, Bryce drank down the last of his cola, crumpled the can, and threw it in the trash.

When he started toward the door, his mother said, "Don't forget your books."

Bryce sighed through his nose and fetched the stack of books from his room. His mother had brought them back with hopes he would catch-up with his schoolwork. He hadn't put forth much effort.

He lugged the books out the door. His mother's word of goodbye sounded distant as he closed the front door.

Richard already sat inside his car, its engine running. Bryce climbed in, thumped his books into the floorboard, and fastened his seat belt. Richard shifted the car into reverse. With a quick look back, he backed up the length of the driveway and onto the street, where he shifted again and drove them to the end of Evelyn Drive. From there they followed Dartmoor, until it merged with Hatch Street.

Bryce watched the storefronts whish past. He switched his gaze downward to the denim of his jeans.

He clenched his hands into fists. His palms were sweating.

Richard kept his eyes on the road and a firm hand on the wheel. He said nothing during the ride until he brought the car to a slow stop in front of the school's front entrance.

"We're here," he said.

Bryce removed his seat belt. He reached to open the car door, but hesitated. He noticed a couple of students standing near the brown front doors. They looked toward him.

"What's wrong?" Richard asked, his tone brisk.

"Nothing," Bryce said, but it was a lie.

He pulled the door's handle, pushed the door open, and eased himself out.

Anybody Want to Play WAR?

"Be careful," Richard said.

Bryce lifted his books and closed the car door with his knee. Richard leaned over to reopen the door and slammed it securely shut.

Richard's Buick accelerated around and along the curving lane to the edge of the school's front lot. There he waited for a few vehicles to pass before turning onto the street and driving away.

The two girls in front of the school's front entrance halted their whispering exchange when Bryce faced them with his arms full of books. One of the girls' eyes widened. Glances passed between the pair.

Bryce moved past them and through the front doors. He hoped he would see Finn but doubted he would be around until the last minute. Bryce was on his own.

He entered the main entry hallway and skirted its edge, keeping his face down. He made a rapid path to his locker and deposited his books.

His bladder was suddenly full. He hurried to the restroom, and to his relief, saw no one else inside. He hurried to a urinal and relieved himself.

He washed his hands with a glob of pink soap from the dispenser and grabbed a couple of brown paper towels to dry off. He considered hiding out in the restroom for a while. Who else would know?

He slipped into the back-corner restroom stall, shut the door, and slid the bolt into place. Feeling trapped, like a caged animal cornered by sadistic zookeepers while countless onlookers watched, he studied the blue-green restroom floor and fought to push his anxiety down.

When the bell rang, it would be time for class—algebra, Mrs. Davenport's class, his first of the day. The first and the worst.

He tensed when someone entered the restroom. He heard a trickle splashing down into a urinal, a flush, and footsteps leaving.

A few more came in, talking, rambling. A couple of kids lingered around longer than he liked.

The bell rang. He froze, startled. Had it been that long?

"Shit," he fired beneath his breath. He mentally braced himself and unlatched the stall door. The restroom had cleared by now, at least, but it wouldn't matter in another minute.

Bryce exited the restroom and hurried along the hallway. He kept his face down until he reached his locker.

Most were already rushing to class. A brown-haired girl hovered at another locker not far from him. At the edge of his vision, he saw her face turn toward him. He felt her eyes studying the prominent red scar that ran down his face.

Bryce forced his attention onto the dial in front of him. He spun it to each number of the combination and yanked at the lock. It didn't open. This exasperated him more than it should have, but he gave it another try, slowly going through each of the numbers again, and this time it opened.

He withdrew his orange hard-backed algebra book and slipped it under his arm, taking a notebook and a pencil along with it. He closed and relocked the locker before making a quick pace down the hallway toward his first class.

"No way," someone said in front of him, a bit louder than normal.

Damn.

"Look at his face."

"A dog did that?"

"That's what I heard."

A couple of others stopped to look. Bryce raised his head and stared at each and every one of them. "You'd better get out of my way, right now," he said.

Close behind him, someone laughed. He turned around and stood nose-to-nose with a blond-haired kid's big-grinning face.

"What's wrong, dog boy?" Nate Plunkett asked. "Forgot to get your face fixed?"

From somewhere among the people around him, Bryce

heard a stifled giggle. He shifted his burning gaze toward its source among the surrounding faces, and he saw Brittany, that girl from Mrs. Davenport's class, trying to hold back her laughter.

Bryce dropped his algebra book, pencils, and paper and hit Nate in his smirking face.

Nate's grin vanished with a burst of blood. He tumbled back and hit the floor.

A girl screamed. Shouts rose. "Fight! Fight! Fight!"

But the fight was over. Nate rolled over and moaned.

Bryce pushed through the crowd, but too many people blocked his way. Thick arms grabbed him and slammed him against the nearest locker.

"You stay right there!" Coach Sikes yelled with a spray of spittle. Bryce squirmed to pull free. The football coach shoved him harder against the locker's surface.

Principal Kaiser shoved through the crowd to help Nate to his feet. Two teachers rushed to assist.

The principal made his way over to Bryce with a steely scowl, and said, "To my office, now!"

II

Bryce sat in one of two folding metal chairs outside the principal's office. The office door was closed. Nate was inside with the principal, dishing out the dirt on Bryce, Bryce assumed.

They had been in there for a while. He couldn't guess what might be taking so long.

On Bryce's left, a potted plant sat on the floor, and a water cooler stood on the other side of it. To his right, the short hall that led him here connected with the school's supply office at its other end.

The compact hall featured only one other door, that to the assistant principal's office. Mr. Crane usually handled these disciplinary matters with students, but Bryce hadn't seen the man since he had returned to school.

Of course, he hadn't been back for long. He hadn't even made it to his first class yet.

Bryce examined the wood grains in the principal's door until the brass knob turned and the door opened. Nate came out. He avoided looking at Bryce. Principal Kaiser, a tall man with meticulous, short brown hair, a brown suit, and glasses, stepped out behind him. The principal addressed Bryce.

"Bryce Gallo, correct? Before we go any further, I want you to apologize to Mr. Plunkett here. You had no reason to do what you did to him."

"But I did have a reason," Bryce said.

"This is the last time I'm going to say it," Kaiser said. "Apologize."

"Sorry," Bryce tossed out, although he wasn't sorry at all and his tone made it obvious.

"Go on to class," Kaiser said to Nate. Nate moved sullenly on.

"You, come in," Mr. Kaiser said to Bryce. "I'm ready to see you in my office."

The principal waited with his hand on the doorknob until Bryce was inside. He closed the door.

"Empty your pockets," Mr. Kaiser said.

Bryce reached into his pocket and pulled out his wadded-up money. He placed it on the edge of the mahogany desk. He slid a hand into his other pocket, dug around, and withdrew his hand.

"Is that it?" Mr. Kaiser asked.

"That's it."

Mr. Kaiser stepped over and patted Bryce's pockets. He stopped when he felt the pocketknife through the denim. "What is this?"

"Nothing."

Mr. Kaiser went into Bryce's right pants-pocket and pulled out the stainless-steel Sterling pocketknife.

"I'll ask you one more time," Mr. Kaiser said. "What is

this?" He held the pocketknife up in clear view.

"You've never seen a pocketknife before?"

Mr. Kaiser walked around his desk. He dropped into the plush black seat behind it and motioned with the pocketknife toward the seat on the opposite side, a less comfortable-looking folding metal chair like the ones outside.

"Sit down," he said.

Bryce took his time in sitting down. Mr. Kaiser rested his elbows against his desk. He held the pocketknife up.

"This is a problem," Mr. Kaiser said. "Do you know why we don't allow weapons in our school?"

The point of this question was to make Bryce look stupid, so he didn't answer.

"Because of students like you," Mr. Kaiser said. "Let me ask you something. I want you to seriously consider it and be honest with your answer. What do you want to be when you grow up?"

The questions weren't getting any better. Bryce would have laughed, but a twinge of tension gave him pause.

He didn't want to go home, he realized, any more than he had wanted to go to school today.

He didn't want to deal with his mother and Richard, or anyone else, and just wanted to be left alone.

"Well?" Mr. Kaiser prompted.

"Do I have to have an answer right now?" Bryce asked. "I have a couple of years till I graduate, don't I?"

"Who says you're going to graduate? You see, for every promising student I see, I also see a student like you. You and I both know you aren't here for an education. You're here because you're told you have to be here, and that's the sum of it. This school is an obstacle to you, not an opportunity, and I don't see things getting better in the future. If you think I'm wrong, I dare you to prove it."

Bryce's eyes roamed across the principal's desk, taking in the black-bordered white calendar lying flat against it, an adjacent stack of papers, and the black ballpoint pen.

Having no argument or enthusiasm for the principal's words, he wanted this meeting to end.

Mr. Kaiser straightened in his seat and put the pocketknife away. "Give it some thought. In the meantime, I'm sending you home with a three-day suspension. I've already called your parents. They are aware of everything. Your mother is on her way."

Bryce sat still, absorbing this. Which was worse, going to school or going home? Out of the frying pan, into another frying pan. The next three days wouldn't be good.

Despite the discomfort bubbling in his stomach, Bryce had a retort. "You're doing me a favor, you know. Three whole days off? It'll be like a vacation."

Mr. Kaiser allowed a wry smile. "Somehow I doubt that."

In this, Bryce knew the principal wasn't wrong. It would be three long, unpleasant days trapped inside his house with his mother and Richard, and they would make those three days horrible for him in any and every way they could. Kaiser knew it almost as well as Bryce did.

Bryce's body felt heavy in the stiff metal chair. He could only think of one more item to address.

"Can I have my pocketknife back?" he asked.

"It will be safe here with me," Mr. Kaiser said.

"My uncle gave it to me. I want it back."

"That won't be possible. There is something very important you should understand here. We have rules, and they will be enforced. If you break the rules, there will be consequences."

Trapped

I

Much like the earlier ride to school, the ride home was quiet and tense. Bryce's mother didn't utter a word.

In Richard's case, it had been expected, but from her it was awful.

"I don't know what Kaiser told you," Bryce said, "but I wasn't the one who started it."

"That's enough."

"I'm just telling you my side of it."

"I said that's enough!" she said, her face flushed. When they reached the driveway of their home, she zipped in and braked hard.

She whirled toward her son. Her curly hair whipped around. Her eyes smoldered with anger.

"We'll talk about it when Richard gets home," she said. "I think we need to have a family discussion."

"If you'd been there today, if you had seen what happened—"

"Save it. Go to your room and stay in there. We'll talk about it later. I haven't told Richard yet. He's still at work and I don't want to ruin his day. We'll have to tell him later. Maybe I'll let you tell him yourself."

"You don't understand," Bryce said. "Look at me. Look what that dog did to me. You think I was ready to step right back into another regular day at school? How could I?"

"I honestly don't want to hear it right now," Elaine said. "You lied to us, and now this. How many times do I have to tell you? Go to your room. We'll talk about it later."

Bryce climbed out of the car and slammed the car door. After his mother unlocked the house's front door, he pushed in past her and down the hallway to his room. He shut the door and switched on his radio.

Before he could find a listenable station, his mother burst into his room. She walked past him, and before he could react, she snatched the radio and jerked the plug out of the wall.

"What are you doing?" he exclaimed.

"I'm taking this," she said. "You're in dangerous waters, and I don't think you realize just how deep."

"I can't even listen to the radio? What am I supposed to do?"

"You should've thought about that before you got yourself kicked out of school. You stay in here and I don't want to hear anything else out of you until Richard gets home. You need to think about what you did and how you're going to explain yourself tonight."

She walked out of the room and closed the door behind her. Bryce almost opened the door and followed her out. He had a lot to say and if he didn't get it out of his system, he might break a window.

Instead, he sat on his bed, sucked in a deep breath, and stewed on it. He had hit Nate Plunkett, that's what had gotten him suspended, but he didn't feel bad about doing it. If the same situation occurred tomorrow, he would do it again, because fuck that goofy bastard.

II

Anybody Want to Play WAR?

Bryce lay on his bed, angry thoughts ricocheting through his mind over the next hours until they made him weary.

He thought back to his incredibly short day at school and Brittany giggling in the hallway after Nate came in with his remarks. Thinking about her made him uncomfortable now. He preferred to think about the women in his stashed magazines. Maybe they weren't real, not in his world, anyway, but they were hot stuff and they didn't giggle when little shitheads poked at him.

He considered digging his magazines out of their hiding space under the vent, but he heard his mother clomping down the hallway. Suspecting she might come back into his room, he left the magazines in their place.

She didn't come in, however, so Bryce continued to lie there, shifting around, dwelling on what had happened at school and how everyone had taken Nate's side without giving him the slightest opening to tell his own side of the story.

No one wanted to hear it. Everyone wanted to accuse and punish.

If people wanted to keep talking about him at school, now they had a real reason. He had given them one in the heat of his shame and anger, but maybe it was better that way. As for poor Nate, who really cared? Not Bryce. He would have a smile on his face about it if he wasn't in two tons of trouble. So what?

Lethargic resignation settled in. He fell asleep and didn't realize as much until the front door's hard thud woke him. The sounds of voices commenced, his mother's and Richard's.

Why wait? He climbed out of bed and walked to the kitchen.

When he emerged into their view, his mother shouted at him. "Get back in your room until we come and get you!"

"That's all right, Elaine," Richard said with frigid calmness. He wore his white collared shirt from work, the tie loosened. "It's better if we address this right now." He looked to Bryce and gestured to one of the kitchen table's chairs. "Sit down."

Bryce pulled back a wooden chair and sat at the table. Richard remained standing. Elaine crossed her arms, her eyes dark with anger and disappointment, and her lips pressed together.

Richard stared down at Bryce. "Tell us what happened today."

"You know what happened," Bryce replied.

"Answer him," his mother said.

"What's to tell?" Bryce said. "Some kid harassed me. I hit him."

"He's suspended from school," Elaine said to Richard. She spun toward Bryce. "You did this on purpose, didn't you? You were trying to get kicked out of school. All this after you missed school yesterday and lied to us!"

"Look at me," Bryce said to both of them. "Look at my face after what that dog did to me. I'll never be the same again. You think it was easy to walk back in there? I knew something would happen, I knew it, but you people never gave a damn."

"Don't you speak to us that way!" Elaine exclaimed.

Richard's voice was low, but clear. "You listen to me," he said to Bryce. "All of this behavior, the fighting, the lying—it stops right here."

Stepping closer, Richard pointed a finger at Bryce. "Your mother is upset. I'm not going to stand by and watch you do this to her anymore. What happened with that dog isn't any excuse for anything. Life can throw harder punches than that. I've gotten up and dusted myself off more times than I can count, and the next day, I went back to work and did what I had to do. You think you have it hard? You have a roof over your head and warm meals, more than a lot of people in the world have. If you don't appreciate what you have around here, that's your own fault."

Richard stood too close for Bryce's comfort. He almost wanted Richard to take a swing at him, because right now, he was thinking he might swing back.

"You want to know why I did what I did?" Bryce asked instead. "Because when you dropped me off at school this morning, I went in expecting the worst, and that's what I got. I didn't even make it to my first class. You expect me to make it through every day without any problems? I already hated school. Now I hate it more."

"You'll wish you were back in school soon enough," Richard said. "Because of what you've done, I'm arranging to take the next three days off from work, and your mother and I are going to stay here and see to it you make the best of your time. You have schoolwork to catch up on, plenty of it from what I understand, and we have work around here that needs to be done. You can count on getting up early. Your mother told me she took your radio. There won't be any more radio, that's right, and you won't be using the phone, watching television, or going anywhere for a long time."

"Except back to school," Elaine added, "when your suspension is up."

"And when I go back," Bryce said, "how long do you think that'll last?"

"If it continues to be a problem," Richard said, his stare never wavering, "there's always military school."

Bryce swung a glance at his mother. She had nodded with Richard's statement, however minimally.

"Go ahead," Bryce said. "Send me away. It gets me out of here, at the very least. I hate this place."

"We've heard enough," Richard said. "If you're going to sit here and argue, you might as well go back to your room."

Bryce ignored Richard and addressed his mother. "You know Mr. Kaiser took my pocketknife?"

"You shouldn't have brought it to school in the first place," Richard said.

"I'm talking to my mom, not you," Bryce said.

"Richard is right," Elaine said.

"That was *my* pocketknife that Uncle Jax gave me. But

you people don't care, I get that. No matter what I did or what really happened, you aren't going to listen to me."

He didn't wait for a response this time. He stood up and went back to his room. Richard was talking, saying something about a busy few days ahead and a lot to think about. Bryce heard it, but he wasn't listening.

III

Bryce smelled dinner cooking, something tomatoey-smelling. His mother stopped by, tapped on his door, and opened it.

"Dinner's ready," she said.

Bryce wasn't hungry. He ignored it. Shortly after, he heard his mother talking in the kitchen. Bryce couldn't quite discern Richard's reply or the quiet exchange afterward.

He waited for his mother to come back to his room, but he didn't hear any footsteps entering the hallway. They ate without him.

Bryce thought of the question Mr. Kaiser had asked him, about what he wanted to be when he grew up. The more he thought of it, the sillier it seemed. Why did the man expect him to have some grand plan? He couldn't even see two days ahead.

With no radio and no distractions but his own thoughts, Bryce stared absently toward the bedroom's single crimson-curtained window.

Soft footsteps sounded in the hallway. Two gentle taps sounded at his door. The doorknob turned and his door opened a tad.

"There's a plate for you on the kitchen counter," his mother said.

Bryce didn't respond.

"I wrapped it in foil," she said. "It's there for whenever you want it."

She shut the door. Bryce stood up, only to turn off the light and return to bed.

Anybody Want to Play WAR?

Over the next hours, when the house went silent and dark, he knew sleep wouldn't come because on some level, the weight of his discontent had tipped the scales and he had reached a new impulse.

Outside the window, wind stirred the leaves of a small tree. Otherwise, the night was still.

Standing up, he pushed between the curtains to peer out the window. He placed a hand on each side of the window and pushed it upward and open. A gentle wind stirred the leaves outside.

He put one leg out the window, then the other, and pushed himself through until he emerged to land on the grassy ground outside. After turning back to close the window, he hurried across the dark lawn and out to the street, where he took his future into his own hands by the light of the moon and stars.

Escape

Headlights came and went. When the street cleared, Bryce ran across.

"Must be nice to have a car," muttered the kid who still rode the bus.

Nate Plunkett's house was somewhere along Dartmoor Street, Bryce thought. He didn't know which house it was, but it couldn't be far. They shared the same bus stop. Wouldn't Nate be surprised if Bryce showed up at the bus stop tomorrow?

It was only a thought. The truth was, that weasel Nate wasn't worth the trouble.

Bryce continued to the next road and into the adjoining neighborhood. He had gone this way yesterday. Tonight, many of the houses were dark.

As he walked, he scanned the hedges and ditches. He almost reached into his pocket for his pocketknife, but remembered it wasn't there. Without it, he felt vulnerable.

He turned down that long street whose name he couldn't remember, stuck his hands into his pockets, and wondered what would happen when his mother discovered he was gone. He hoped she hadn't yet. The thought that he could still turn back, climb back through the window and into his room, came as a faint reassurance.

A dog roared from the dark. He stumbled back, pulled his hands from his pockets in an awkward hurry, and curled them into fists.

A chain held the dog back, he realized, and remembered this dog had frightened him before. His subsiding fear left him angry.

He leaned down, grabbed a rock, and flung it. The rock sailed wide of the dog and toward the house. A window shattered.

The dog fought against its chain, barking. A light came on in the house. Bryce ran like crazy.

The front door swung open. A balding man in a white, red-striped robe stepped out, yelled at his dog to shut up, and glared around in search of the vandal.

Bryce was already well down the street. He ran for everything he was worth, which might not be much, but it saved him a beating tonight.

He recalled the old kick-the-can-hating man who had warned him never to step on his property again. When he saw the man's white house with the unoccupied green stool against its front facade, he cut across the lawn.

He anticipated a confrontation but didn't see the man around. He raced to the back of the property, bordered by dense brush, and found a narrow trail through the brush. He pushed through. On the other side, he emerged into a ditch on one side of Hatch Street.

He slowed to a walk along the roadside and caught his breath. What now? He wasn't sure, but as he walked and the sparse late traffic hummed past him, he had an idea.

II

Tuck's corner store was still open. Bryce passed it.

Ahead, he could see the dimly lit parking lot of the

apartment building. He saw three cars parked there. Only one of the apartments' lights were on, he noticed once closer, the one on the upstairs left.

He remembered the morning of the previous day when he had met those two over here, Wheels and what's-her-name, the woman who hadn't said much. Wheels had mentioned something about someone clearing out of one of these apartments. He only wished he could remember which number. It was either #2 or #4, or maybe #3.

He scanned the building's four doors, two downstairs and two upstairs, but couldn't see any numbers. He moved closer to one of the apartments, the lower-left one. After another moment's search, his eyes found an unobtrusive #1 darkly painted against the gray exterior next to the door.

He crossed over to the apartment marked as #2. A fuzzy brown mat lay in front of this apartment's front door. He continued to the nearby concrete steps and climbed up the two flights to the apartment above, #4, which was dark and silent.

Was this the one? He hoped so. He gave the front door three soft knocks and waited. No one answered.

He tried the door's knob. It was locked.

He looked down to the lot and out to the street. He didn't see anyone watching.

He tried the window. It came partly open, but stuck. Bryce anchored both hands on the bottom of the window panel and heaved upward. With some resistance, it came open.

He pushed aside the yellow curtain within and looked in but couldn't see a thing in the dark interior.

He climbed in and closed the window behind him. His fingers found the latch mechanism at the top and secured it.

He took soft steps in the darkness, his arms outstretched to feel for obstacles. After several uncertain steps through the black space, his hand brushed a wall. He ran his hands along it and found a doorway. He felt along its edges for a light switch, but in vain.

With both hands on the doorway frame, he maneuvered around it and probed the section of wall on the other side. This time, he found a switch and flipped it by accident. The light came on. A bare kitchen sprang into view.

Bryce held his breath. There remained a possibility he had the wrong apartment, and that any second, some furious tenant would bum-rush him out of nowhere and beat him to the floor, or worse, shoot him.

Seconds rolled by, and no such thing occurred.

He crossed the empty yellow kitchen to the opposite doorway, which led into a short forum connecting a bedroom and bathroom. By the scarce light from the kitchen, the bedroom appeared empty as well, without even a bed inside.

Bryce flipped the bedroom's light on. The place was empty. He switched the light off again and proceeded to the bathroom.

It was a basic, functional bathroom with a toilet, sink, and white-curtained shower. He pushed the curtain aside, gave the shower a quick inspection, and returned to the kitchen.

Besides a bedroom closet, the only other space in the apartment was the room he had first entered, as empty as the rest of the place. As for the closet, it revealed only four close white walls and several hanging clothes-hangers.

He allowed himself to relax. This was the right apartment, the empty one, the one for Bryce—at least for tonight.

He returned to the kitchen to turn off the kitchen light and left only the bathroom's light on. He didn't need anyone seeing the lights on in here. Having the apartment to himself tonight, he wanted it to stay that way.

He huddled into a corner of the bedroom and leaned back against a wall. A trickle of light from the bathroom filtered in.

He could hardly believe his idea had worked. For now, he had achieved silence and solitude. He hadn't breathed this easily in weeks, not since before that dog had attacked him.

But even with tonight's peace, Bryce remained restless, his mind filled with disastrous possibilities of the day to come. He wished he had a cigarette.

Loveless

Bryce snapped awake in an exhausted confusion with someone screaming at him. "You little shit!"

Rough hands hauled him to his feet, tearing his shirt in the process, and shoved him. He stumbled, his shoulder struck the side of the bedroom's door frame, and he spun to the floor.

Before he could fully climb back to his feet, his aggressor shoved him again. He sprawled into the forum.

"Get your ass up! Get up and get out of here!"

As Bryce tried to scramble to his feet again, the man seized him by the back of his shirt and propelled him into the living room. This time, Bryce managed to catch his balance. He whirled to confront his aggressor.

He faced a heavyset bald man in a sweat-stained, light-blue collared shirt, a crooked tie, and slacks. The man clenched a fist and, with his other hand, pointed an accusing finger at Bryce.

"You get the hell out of here," he said.

Bryce sifted partly through his confusion to retrieve a jumbled recollection of where he was and why he was here, but at the forefront of everything, this guy pissed him off. He wanted a fight? That's what he'd get.

Bryce lunged for a swing. Before Bryce could land his shot, the man struck fast. Bryce twisted to dodge. The blow glanced the side of his head. The man followed in with a fast jab that sent Bryce to the living room carpet. An ache fired through his head, but he wasn't finished yet. He lurched back to his feet.

The man shook the last punch from his thick knuckles and stepped forward. Rage hardened his eyes.

"Shithead," Bryce muttered.

The man rushed at him. Again, he was quicker than Bryce anticipated. Before Bryce could evade, the man's arm caught him and barreled him backward through the apartment's front door. Both of them tumbled against the second-floor railing.

The rail shook. Bryce shoved against the man's bulk, but to no avail. The man had him pinned against the unsteady rail, which quivered and threatened to give out at any instant. He couldn't gain much leverage while trapped this way, not until with a rumbling snarl, the man shifted and freed his arms to grab Bryce by the front of his shirt.

Bryce's next thought was to nail the bastard in the nose with a solid punch, but someone shouted from the parking lot below.

"Loveless, let him go, man!"

The man's grip loosened. Bryce slipped free and ducked out of the man's reach, maneuvering toward the stairway. The big man, Loveless, looked over the rail toward the source of the voice.

"This punk's got a lesson to learn," he declared, and returned his attention to Bryce, but Bryce had taken to the stairs.

"Come on and get me, idiot," he called, and Loveless immediately launched down the stairs after him. At the bottom of the steps, Bryce turned to face his looming pursuer.

"Whoa, Mr. Loveless, you gotta relax," Wheels said,

almost daring to come between them, but clearly reluctant to intercept Loveless's anger with his body.

Loveless jabbed a finger in Bryce's direction. "I caught him up there in #4! He broke in. I ought to call the cops on this little asshole!"

"What were you doing in there?" the woman who accompanied Wheels, now dressed in blue-and-white garb, asked Bryce. Her name suddenly returned to him: Paloma.

Bryce backed up a step. "Look, I'm sorry," he said. "I just needed a place to stay for a night. Wheels said that one was empty."

Loveless jerked around to face Wheels. "You know this punk?" he exclaimed. "I swear, if you're responsible for this in any way, I'll fire your ass so fast it'll make your head spin."

"He didn't do anything," Bryce said. "I did it. I heard him talking about it, and I needed a place to stay. That's it. Then you showed up going crazy."

"I wasn't talking to you!" Loveless spat. "I'm talking to Jones here. What about it, Jones? Is that about right? You had a hand in this, didn't you?"

It took a second for Bryce to recall that Wheels's actual name was Jones.

"I didn't do a damned thing," Wheels said.

Paloma stepped near Bryce. "You're bleeding," she assessed. "Come on. We need to get that cleaned up."

Loveless's glare switched from Wheels to Bryce again. "I think I have a good idea of what's going on here," he said. "Jones here said it would be all right for you to stay around here rent-free, didn't he? We'll see about that. None of you rat-shit scumbags have any idea what you've gotten yourselves into, but you're about to find out." He pushed past them.

Several steps across the lot, he stopped to turn around and point at Wheels. "You might as well pack it up, Jones. You're finished around here." He swung his attention back to Bryce. "And I better not ever see your ass around here again."

He resumed his walk toward a white car that appeared

too small for him. Paloma looked to Wheels, her expression neutral, while Wheels pointed his glare at Bryce and exclaimed, "What in the hell were you thinking?"

"Sorry," Bryce said with a shrug.

Loveless's car door slammed. He squealed out of the parking lot.

Paloma took Bryce by the arm and led him toward one of the apartments, the lower-left one, #1. Wheels muttered behind him.

"Crazy," he said. "The man comes up here yelling at me like I had anything to do with it. What are you trying to do, boy, get me into a whole lot of trouble?"

"I didn't know it would cause that much trouble," Bryce said as they stepped onto the soft brown carpet of Paloma's apartment. While Wheels scowled at Bryce, Paloma went to her bathroom.

Bryce first noticed the tiled mirror hanging on the left wall of the living room, then the brown couch with a folded green-and-gray patterned blanket on one end. To Bryce's right, a long tapestry of swirled blue, beige, and gold adorned the center of the wall.

Paloma reentered the room with a white washcloth, which she placed in Bryce's hand. "Here," she said. Bryce pressed it to his face. When he wiped it against his nose, it came away with a smear of blood.

"I guess he got me," Bryce said.

"You know who that was?" Wheels asked.

"Some asshole," Bryce said.

"George Loveless," Wheels said. "The property manager."

"That's your boss?"

"Yeah."

"Damn, Wheels, I'm sorry. I didn't mean to cause that much of a problem."

"It's already done," Wheels said. Some of the agitation slid from his expression, but he shook his head. He pulled out his pack of cigarettes and removed one.

"I gotta have a smoke," he said, and went outside.

Bryce wanted a smoke, too, but decided it wasn't the best time to ask.

He stepped outside after Wheels. "I thought that apartment was empty," he said. "I thought it would be okay to stay there for one night."

Wheels smoked his cigarette and stared to the other side of the street. With his silence, the blame weighed heavier on Bryce's shoulders.

"After I finish my cigarette," Wheels eventually said, "I got a phone call to make."

II

Once Wheels smoked the cigarette down to its filter, he extinguished it against the ground and said, "Wait here." He went upstairs and into his apartment.

Paloma waited outside her apartment with Bryce. "What's the real reason you came back here?" she asked.

"Nowhere else to go," Bryce said.

Paloma scrutinized him as she had when they had first met. Bryce felt the familiar discomfort of that meeting returning. She knew he was lying. He knew it and she knew it. He almost wished she would say it so he could try to refute the accusation, but she stood in silence, her mind dissecting his words and her eyes probing through his facade.

Wheels's apartment door swung open. He stepped outside, threw the door shut behind him, and anchored his hands against the rail.

"Tried calling two times," Wheels said to Paloma from above. "Couldn't get through."

"What do you want to do?" she asked.

"It looks like we have to make a special trip. Loveless will have his say, I know that much. I'd better get mine in while I have the chance."

"Do you want me to drive you?" Paloma asked.

"Yeah," Wheels said. "That'd be good."

He came down the stairs. When he reached the bottom, he paused with a hand on the rail and looked to Bryce. "You want to do something to make this right?"

"I'll do what I can," Bryce said.

"Then you need to come along with us." Wheels crossed the lot toward a small, dusty brown car, a hatchback. Paloma fell in after him.

After a cursory inspection of the subcompact vehicle, Bryce had to ask, "How are we all supposed to fit inside this thing?"

"You said you wanted to help out, right?" Wheels replied. "Climb up in the back. You'll fit."

Paloma unlocked the car for them. She settled into the driver's side and started the engine. Wheels hopped into the passenger's side. Bryce squeezed into the back of the car. He pulled the rear door shut and gave it a fair slam. Without sufficient leg room, he struggled to adjust. This was bound to be an uncomfortable ride.

"Where are we going?" he asked.

"We're going to try to save my job," Wheels said. "So you need to think about what happened back there with Loveless, because you're gonna have a lot of explaining to do."

A Special Trip

I

Scrunched into the rear compartment of Paloma's car, Bryce said, "He started it."

"You weren't supposed to be there," Wheels said. "That's breaking and entering, you realize that?"

"I didn't break anything," Bryce said. "How can be it breaking and entering?"

"You know damn well you didn't belong in there," Wheels said. "You want to start living there, you gotta pay rent. That's the way it works."

Paloma's car fired between a speckling of old white houses on each side of Hatch Street. They passed a warehouse on the left side, and farther ahead on the right, a mostly abandoned strip mall.

After they passed a liquor store farther along, the road became bumpier, jostling Bryce in the back. He shifted again but couldn't find a comfortable position.

"Where did you say we were going again?" he asked. Before Wheels or Paloma could respond, another thought sprang into his mind. "If Loveless is your boss and he wants to fire you, how are we supposed to stop him?"

"Loveless is the manager," Wheels said, "but he's not

61

the owner. That's who we're going to see. I hope we can fix this. Loveless might not be the easiest man to get along with, I'll give you that, but you shouldn't have pissed him off."

"I didn't do anything."

"Yeah, you did. You might as well get all those lying ideas out of your head right now."

Bryce looked out the window again. Now they passed Candle Square with its jam-packed assortment of bars, clubs, and hole-in-the-wall restaurants. There wasn't much business around during the day, but at night, especially on Fridays and Saturdays, people would swarm in from the streets, hungry, thirsty, and looking for a distraction.

Then they moved beyond Candle Square and past Summerset Park to push deeper into east downtown St. Charles.

The car slowed for a right turn. Down this strip, graffiti marked structures of gray and brown brick: gibberish, threats, genitalia. Across various areas, 7's were spray-painted in green and black. A bold black *777* garnished the front of a boarded-up, mint-green brick building.

A memory of the old neighborhood entered Bryce's thoughts.

As a young child, he had once wandered up his street on the east side of downtown, north of Hatch Street, where three teenagers watched him from the corner. One sat on the cracked sidewalk, another leaned against the stop sign, and the last, a tall, skinny kid, spoke to him.

"What you doing over here, boy?"

"Walking," Bryce said.

The lanky one looked over at the one leaning on the sign. "Says he's walking."

The one by the sign, shorter with a wide mouth and a pug-like nose, chuckled.

"You ought to be careful where you walk," the tall kid said to Bryce.

"Why?" Bryce asked.

Anybody Want to Play WAR?

"Sometimes bad things happen to kids who don't pay attention where they're going," the tall kid said. "I'd watch out if I was you."

That was the end of the exchange, but those three watched him all the way back to his house up the street.

Later that night, the smashing of glass startled him. Uncle Jax stood from the recliner. Bryce came up from the couch, but his mother pulled him back.

"Stay here," Elaine whispered, fearful.

Uncle Jax already had a few whiskeys in him. He went into his bedroom at the back of the house and brought his rifle into the living room.

Elaine's face was pale. She clung to Bryce, both arms firmly around him.

Uncle Jax, wearing his green army jacket and holding his rifle in both hands, stepped onto the front porch.

Three figures scattered down the street. Bryce remembered the three teenagers on the corner then, the ones who had warned him to be careful.

Uncle Jax remained on the front porch for at least another five minutes, his rifle in his hands, its sling dangling.

A neighbor's car across the street had been broken into, its windows smashed, and tires slashed, they later learned.

Years after, when Bryce's mother married Richard, Jax's rifle was one of the items sold at their neighborhood sale before their move to the new home.

II

The car pulled into the smoothly paved driveway of a large red-brick house.

Paloma and Wheels exited the car. Bryce fumbled at the rear hatch door but couldn't get it open. He readjusted his position to gain a better view of the house.

Behind the gate and tall black bars of the property's fence, the driveway extended to the house to meet dual white garage doors, both closed.

Wheels tried the gate, but a chain and padlock secured it. He took the gate's padlock in his hand and asked, "How are we supposed to get in to see her?"

"I don't think we are," Paloma said. "Not without calling first."

"I tried," Wheels said. "A couple of times."

"We don't know for sure if she's even home," Paloma said. She lifted her gaze toward the house.

Wheels released the padlock. "What now?"

By this time, Bryce had wormed his way through the space between the rear compartment and seats. He slid into the passenger's seat and rolled down a window.

"What's wrong?" he called out the window.

"Gate's locked," Wheels answered. "And we don't know if anybody's home."

Bryce honked the car's horn. In unison, the other two cast sharp glances at him.

"Hey!" Wheels shouted. He briskly walked to the passenger's side window. "What are you trying to do?"

"Get somebody's attention," Bryce said.

"You can't be doing that," Wheels said. "You're gonna piss somebody off right away, you know that? That's not what we need right now."

Paloma's head turned back toward the house, Bryce noticed. The front door had opened. Wheels, noticing Bryce's attention had diverted to the house, also looked.

A thin woman in a white Oxford shirt, with red hair in a ponytail, emerged to walk down the front steps and approach the gate. Her narrow green eyes took in Wheels and Paloma before roaming toward the car where Bryce sat.

Paloma met her at the gate. A low exchange passed between them. Wheels returned to the gate, but by the time he neared it, the red-haired woman walked away.

"What's going on?" Wheels asked Paloma.

"I told her why we're here," Paloma replied. She motioned

her head toward the car and called to Bryce, "Come on out."

Bryce opened the driver's side door and climbed out. He slammed the door and joined Paloma and Wheels at the gate.

Soon the house's front door reopened. The red-haired woman came outside again and stopped at the gate to study Bryce in silence.

Discomfort rose in him. He remembered the horrible scar on his face, something he hadn't even considered between the events of the previous night and this morning. He almost turned from the woman's gaze, but a simmering defiance overrode his discomfort and he matched her stare.

He almost dared her to make a remark about his face, but when she spoke, she only asked, "Who are you?"

"Bryce."

"Do you have a last name, Bryce?"

He didn't care to give his full name, not his real one. "Stafford," he lied.

It was the first name that came to mind, his mother's maiden name and Uncle Jax's last name. His true last name, Gallo, was a souvenir from a man he never knew.

If Paloma knew he was lying this time, she didn't betray it, but she wasn't looking at him. The woman at the gate nodded. She shuffled an item around in her hands, a ring of keys, and inserted one into the padlock to pop it open. She unwrapped the chain and eased the gate open.

"Come in," she said.

She watched each of them pass through the opening. Once they were in, she replaced the chain and lock.

She gestured toward the house. "Go ahead," she said, and they continued up the driveway.

Square-trimmed hedges bordered each side of the few broad steps preceding the house's front door of polished cherry oak. Paloma paused there. Wheels stopped behind her.

"Go on in," their gate-greeter said. "She knows you're here."

Inside, they crossed a round crimson rug to the hardwood floor of a foyer. Two decorative paintings adorned the walls, but they were hard to discern in the lack of illumination. An unused soft white fixture hung above.

The foyer met a larger room where the only lighting stemmed from a small lamp on a round stand in a far-right corner. Two white sofas graced this room, with a low polished wooden coffee table between them. In the opposite left corner, another round wooden stand supported a record player. Near it, a plush crimson barrel chair sat with its back to the wall.

A woman in a red blouse, her brown hair wavy and abundant, appeared from the arch-like doorway to their left side. The room's steep dimness shrouded her features. Her hands cradled a white ceramic cup.

"Good morning," she said. "I have coffee and tea in the kitchen. Would any of you care for some?"

"No, thank you," Paloma said.

"I'm good, but thanks," Wheels said.

The woman glanced to Bryce. "I'm sorry, we haven't met. Or have we? I'm Tabby Reinhart."

"Bryce Stafford." Again, he withheld his actual last name.

Tabby merely nodded and returned her attention to Wheels and Paloma. "It's been a while," she said.

"Thank you for seeing us," Paloma said.

"Of course. Now, we can do this here, or we can go into the study, whichever you would prefer."

"This is fine," Paloma said.

Tabby motioned to one of the sofas. "Have a seat."

Wheels and Paloma took a seat on the sofa. Bryce sat down on the other. Tabby pulled the room's single chair over and slid into it. She leaned forward, her hands retaining the white cup.

"Now, what is this about?" she asked.

"I know it's early," Wheels said. "I didn't want to bother you with this, but I didn't know what else to do. We had a problem this morning out at 2803." He hesitated. "A problem named George Loveless."

"What happened?" Tabby asked.

With a glance at Paloma, Wheels recounted his version of the morning's events, starting with witnessing the violent exchange on the upper level of the apartment building and finishing with Loveless's threats and furious exit.

"Do you two actually know each other?" Tabby asked Wheels, nodding toward Bryce.

"We met just one time before," Wheels said. "But I didn't have a thing to do with him being up there in that apartment."

Tabby shifted her legs, crossing one over the other. She directed her attention to Bryce. "Why were you in the apartment to begin with?" she asked.

"I didn't have anywhere else to go," he replied.

A length of silence met Bryce's response. He hurried on to add, "I would've left in the morning. I only needed a few hours' sleep. I heard Wheels say something about people clearing out of that apartment. He didn't know I would do what I did. It isn't his fault."

But Wheels was looking at him now, and something wasn't quite right. Bryce was uncertain until Wheels said, "Nowhere else to go? I thought you told me you lived over on the west side."

Bryce realized his mistake and hastily amended, "Not anymore." When they continued to look at him, he added, "It's a long story."

This seemed the easiest method of diverting the conversation. For now, it appeared to work. Wheels rubbed his hands together. Some of the tension eased from his posture, but not all of it.

"You do realize you shouldn't have done what you did?" Tabby asked Bryce.

Before he could answer, she went on to say, "Don't do it again and I don't think we'll have a problem in the future. If I leave it at that, can we agree to move on with the understanding that this will not happen again?"

Wheels stared at Bryce. Bryce answered, "I think so."

"Good," Tabby said. "Because if it does happen again, Mr. Loveless will be within his rights to call the police."

"Got it," Bryce said.

"I'll call Mr. Loveless," Tabby said. "He shouldn't have attacked you the way he did, by the way, and I don't mind telling him so. I hope he didn't seriously injure you."

"He tried," Bryce said, "but no. I'm just fine. You can tell him so. Tell him I said hello."

Wheels shot Bryce a glare. Tabby seemed not to notice. She stood up.

"I'll call him," she said to the three, "and we'll wrap this up. Give me a minute?"

"Sure," Wheels said. With the cup still in one hand, Tabby crossed the room to pass through the rounded doorway she had first emerged from.

"What's wrong with you?" Wheels whispered to Bryce.

"What's the problem?" Bryce asked. "I just saved your job, didn't I?"

"You're the one who almost cost me my job," Wheels countered. "And don't be trying to stir up a bunch more shit with George Loveless, either."

"Okay, sorry," Bryce said. "Damn."

They heard Tabby on the phone now. "Hello, George? This is Tabby. Yes, I know. No, I haven't been answering the phone. I've had my hands full. Yes, I'm aware. Yes. They're right here. I've been talking to them." After this, Tabby fell into a long period of silence, during which Bryce studied his dim surroundings.

Pictures hung on the walls, it appeared, but he couldn't easily tell what any of them were. Why did Tabby keep the lights so low? And what had happened to the red-headed woman who had let them through the gate? She had disappeared after letting them into the house.

"George, listen to me," Tabby's voice sounded from the

other room. "I'm not firing anyone." There came another pause on her end.

"That's enough," she said, her voice firming. "I'm not going to stand here and listen to this. I think it's best you take the next couple of days off. I'll handle everything until then. Do we have an understanding?" She paused again. "Hello?"

A moment later, Bryce, Wheels, and Paloma heard the click of the phone onto the receiver. Tabby reappeared without her white cup, flustered, Bryce imagined, though he still couldn't see her face well in the darkened house.

"Everything all right?" Wheels asked.

"He didn't take it well," Tabby said. "I'm giving him some time to think it over. In the meantime, don't worry about anything." She reclaimed her seat.

"Sorry for the trouble," Wheels said.

"Mr. Loveless can be a handful to deal with sometimes," Tabby said. "He's thorough at his job and makes my life easier in ways, but—" She carefully considered the words upon her lips, but instead, she shook her head. "I'll deal with him. Don't worry."

"Thanks," Wheels said.

"Is there anything else I can do?"

"I guess that's it," Wheels said. "It sounds like you've got it all under control."

"You can call me if you have any more problems," Tabby said. She stood. "I'll try to answer the phone next time."

"I'd better go," Wheels said. "I have some more work to do over at 5808."

"Right," Tabby said.

"You have time to drop me off over there, right?" Wheels asked Paloma.

"I think we can do that," she replied. The two of them started toward the door. Bryce walked after them until Tabby addressed him.

"Bryce. It is Bryce, right? I hope you don't mind my asking, but how old are you?"

Bryce turned to face her. "Eighteen," he lied, a lie he had told more than once in the past days.

"Where are you going after this?" she asked.

"I don't know. Not back to that empty apartment, for sure."

"You said you didn't have anywhere else to go. Do you mind telling me why?"

Bryce threw together a hasty lie. "They raised the rent at my last place," he said. "I couldn't afford to pay it."

"Maybe we can work something out. If you need work, I can always use some extra help. That's how it started with Wheels. Would you be interested?"

"What kind of work?"

"Facility maintenance. Cutting grass, cleaning up sites, odd jobs, general upkeep. Maybe some painting. Would you be up to it?"

Bryce thought about it. Anything beat going back home, or to school, and if he really meant to try to make it on his own somehow, he needed money.

"You know, I might just take you up on that," he said.

"Good," Tabby said. "Call George Loveless about it. He usually handles that sort of thing."

Bryce stared at her.

"That's a joke," she said. "Don't call George. Please. Just call over here and talk to me when you've made your decision, or if you're ready now, we can go over some things, but I'll need you to fill out some paperwork. It's how the process works, understand."

"Sure," Bryce said, having no clue about any of it.

"You two can go on ahead if you want," Tabby said to Wheels and Paloma, who waited at the foyer. "I'll give him a ride back later, or I'll have Cheryl do it."

Where *back* meant was anyone's guess, but Wheels nodded and headed out. Looking at Bryce, Paloma said, "Take care, Tabby."

"Bye," Tabby said.

Anybody Want to Play WAR?

They opened the front door and the outdoor light flooded in. Tabby stood clear of it, Bryce noticed.

"Cheryl?" she called. The red-haired woman from earlier reappeared from another dark doorway.

"Can you unlock the gate and let them out?" Tabby asked. Cheryl nodded, took out the key ring, and accompanied Wheels and Paloma down the steps. Bryce walked outside, both to see them off and because he was tired of sitting in the dark for no known reason.

Once Cheryl unlocked the padlock, removed the chain, and opened the gate, Paloma and Wheels returned to the car.

"Good luck, little man," Wheels called to Bryce. Bryce winced.

As Paloma's car backed out of the driveway, Bryce returned to the house's front steps and reentered the dark house.

A Dark House

Tabby led Bryce across the foyer and through the arched doorway on their left, past what he thought might be a dining area with a long, dark wooden table and another unlit hanging fixture above. Ahead, this room curved toward the right, into a smaller section which ended at a bar stocked with a variety of liquors and a circular wooden rack of hanging glasses. The only illumination here was a soft-white nightlight plugged into a wall receptacle.

Tabby took a seat beside the bar and motioned to another stool two seats over. "Have a seat," she said, and Bryce accepted the indicated stool.

"Cheryl?" Tabby called. "I'm going to try him for the facility maintenance spot. Can you bring an application in?"

Bryce looked back for Cheryl, but she was already gone. It didn't take long for her to return with two white sheets of paper. She placed them on the bar in front of Bryce and made a wordless departure.

"When you're finished with that, I'll also need to see some ID," Tabby said.

Bryce had no identification, but he would worry about that issue when they came to it. He considered saying he dropped it during the scuffle with George Loveless. That might buy him some time.

He definitely wanted a driver's license, and a car, too, but his mother didn't seem to think it was important and Richard didn't have the patience. Both of them felt Bryce had bigger matters to worry about, like improving his grades in school.

He squinted down at the papers. "It's hard to see in here," he said. "Can we turn the lights on?"

An uncomfortable silence answered him. Bryce kept staring at the application.

"All right," Tabby said, her tone subdued, and she stood. Bryce felt a touch of guilt for even asking, but had he really said anything wrong? It didn't make much sense.

Tabby moved around the bend. She flicked a switch and three lights sprang on above the bar.

"I'll leave you alone to fill that out," Tabby said. She slipped away, leaving Bryce to himself.

"Can I get a pen?" Bryce called. "Something to write with?"

From outside the house, a horn blared. When the impatient visitor blasted the horn several more times, Bryce's curiosity prompted him to stand and made a path back to the house's living room. Tabby and Cheryl were there, Tabby hanging back and Cheryl going for the front door.

"Is somebody here?" Bryce asked. No one answered him.

He drifted to the foyer. Cheryl opened the door and went outside. Bryce blinked against the sudden flood of sunlight.

Before Cheryl shut the door behind her, Bryce glimpsed a small, familiar white car parked beyond the gate. A big bald man in khaki pants and a light-blue button-up shirt stood outside the gate—George Loveless.

"What the hell?" Bryce wondered aloud. He followed Cheryl outside.

"Wait," Tabby spoke, but Bryce walked down the front steps.

Anybody Want to Play WAR?

Cheryl made no hurry in walking to the gate. George Loveless stood with his hands on the padlocked chain. When Cheryl came closer, he gripped the gate's bars.

"What do you need?" Cheryl asked.

"I'm here to talk to her," Loveless said, "not you. Open the gate."

He turned his eyes toward the house and froze when he saw Bryce near the base of the front steps.

"Who the hell is that?" Loveless asked. "Is that the bastard who broke into the apartment this morning? What's he doing here?"

"If you want to talk to Tabby, you can leave a message with me," Cheryl said to Loveless.

"Unlock the gate," Loveless said.

Cheryl visibly lost her cool. "Get lost," she said, "or we'll call the police."

"You want to call the cops?" Loveless raised his voice. "Call the cops, bitch! I'll tell them what that little punk did. They'll arrest his ass! You think you can disrespect me? I bust my ass for that bitch every day! You tell her if she wants to fire me, she can come out here and do it right to my face!"

Cheryl brushed past Bryce on her way back to the house. Bryce walked toward the gate. He couldn't resist.

"Hey, Loveless, how's it going, buddy?" he greeted.

"Fuck you!" Loveless shouted.

The house's front door opened again. Tabby stepped into the light for the first time since Bryce had met her. She blinked several times against the sunlight before coming down the steps.

When she neared him, Bryce saw her face plainly for the first time. Brown eyes, brown hair, her countenance pleasant enough, elegant even, except for a slightly crooked nose.

She didn't return Bryce's watchful gaze, but she swallowed as she walked by and didn't meet his eyes.

"You need to go home, George," she said to the man at the gate.

"Fucking make me, bitch!" he shouted at her. Tabby stepped back, startled.

"I don't have to stand here and listen to this," she said. "I've tried to be patient with you, but you have some serious problems. You come to my home and speak to me this way? I don't think so. It's over, George. You're fired. Don't come around my house again."

"You're fucking Jones, that's it, isn't it?" Loveless said. "You like sucking that black cock?"

"If you're not gone in five minutes," Tabby said, "I will call the police." She turned away and walked back toward the house.

"Or maybe you're fucking this little kid here!" Loveless yelled after her. "Maybe I should call the cops on *you,* you sick bitch! Get a nose job!"

From there, it deteriorated into borderline nonsensical shouting, ranting, and cursing. Bryce stood watching the display for a moment, but with Tabby going back into her house, he decided he should do the same. Before he went back in, he flashed Loveless a smile and flipped him off.

II

Tabby went straight to the bar. In passing, she flicked the bar lights off. She collapsed onto a stool and dropped her head into her arms against the bar's wooden surface.

"Are you all right?" Bryce asked her. She didn't answer for a long time.

"I need a moment," she said at last.

"Tabby?" Cheryl spoke from the dining area. She came around the corner. "Do you want me to call the police?"

"No." Tabby's folded arms muffled her voice. She raised her head and wiped her eyes. "It's okay."

"Want me to go back out there and tell him to fuck off?" Bryce offered.

"Don't worry about it," Tabby replied. "Let him stand out

there and scream his head off. I could use a drink."

Cheryl maneuvered behind the bar. "I'm on it, boss," she said. "Pick your poison."

A screeching of tires sounded outside. Loveless was leaving.

"I'll have a martini," Tabby said.

"One Tabby-style martini, coming up," Cheryl said.

She fetched ice, poured from a square bottle into a cocktail shaker, gave the shaker a gentle double-nudge, and poured the drink into a martini glass for Tabby. Tabby nodded her gratitude and took a sip.

"What's in a Tabby-style martini?" Bryce asked.

"Double gin, extra dry, no olive," Cheryl said. She revisited the shelf for another bottle.

Bryce sat on the stool he had previously occupied. "I'll have the same," he said.

"Not for you, youngster," Cheryl said. She poured a drink for herself, a top-shelf whiskey on ice.

She poured one other drink, ginger ale over ice, and slid it to Bryce. He wasn't impressed. Cheryl took the stool on the other side of Tabby.

"It seems dark in here," Bryce remarked. He didn't touch his ginger ale. Tabby studied him, taking another longer sip of her martini.

"What's wrong with that?" she asked.

"It seems weird, that's all."

"Weird? You know why I keep the lights turned down."

"I have no idea," Bryce said.

"Are you joking?"

"If I am, I'm not doing a very good job. I don't hear anybody laughing."

Cheryl's ice clinked in her short glass. She wasn't talking, only listening as she nursed her whiskey.

Tabby gave a quiet reply. "You've seen the way I look."

"There's nothing wrong with the way you look," Bryce said. Tabby went silent again. It wasn't an uncomfortable silence this time, but a thoughtful one.

Tabby sipped her drink again and carefully placed her glass on the bar. "Thank you for saying so."

"You've seen me, too," Bryce said. "You've seen my scar. Nobody can miss it. I have to learn to live with it. It isn't easy, but what can I do about it? Not a lot."

Tabby looked long at her martini. Without looking over, she asked, "I hope you don't mind my asking, but how did it happen?"

"A dog came after me. The craziest, meanest dog I've ever seen. It put me in the hospital."

"I'm sorry."

"With the look in that dog's eyes, it wouldn't have stopped until it got somebody. It had already killed a man. I found that out later. If it hadn't gotten to me, it probably would've gotten somebody else."

Tabby raised her glass for another drink. Only a small portion remained. Cheryl finished her whiskey and leaned over.

"Want another?" she murmured to Tabby. Tabby nodded. She drained the last of her own drink and pushed the glass over. Cheryl removed their glasses and retrieved the gin to pour another martini for Tabby.

"If you live life long enough," Tabby said to Bryce, "you're bound to pick up a scar or two along the way. Some of them are harder to hide than others."

"I have a scar I can't hide," Bryce said, "but I don't see what's wrong with the way you look."

"I was in a car wreck last year. It gave me an awful concussion and broke my nose. I haven't looked the same since. People notice. You heard what George said about me."

"He's a jackass."

"I never used to think about the way I looked," Tabby said. "Not the way I do now. For years, I guess I was happy with myself, but when people look at me now, I almost feel like I should apologize."

"Is that why you hide inside a dark house?"

"I turn the lights down when someone new comes over, like you," she said, "I'm sorry. I just feel uncomfortable."

"But now I've seen you in the light," Bryce said. "Can I be honest? I like the way you look."

"Thank you. That's a sweet thing to say."

"You don't have to act like a vampire around me anymore. Can we turn the lights on?"

Tabby chuckled. "Have it your way."

She shifted to stand, but Cheryl said, "I'll get it."

Cheryl gathered her glass of melting ice, turned the bar's lights on, and left. "I'll be in here if you need anything, Tabby," she called.

After another minute, Bryce asked quietly, "So what about Cheryl? Is she your assistant?"

"That's right. I hired her last year, when I stopped going out as much. She does a lot to help me out. She's a friend as well as an assistant."

"That's good."

"It is. After everything happened, the quake, my wreck, I realized how alone I was here in St. Charles, even surrounded by people I considered my friends. I used to host parties here every so often. Not anymore. Sometimes I feel like I've become a stranger here. Things aren't the same for a lot of people, I realize that. I probably got off easy. A lot of people's luck ran out on that day of the quake."

She paused for a drink of her fresh martini. "I've noticed," she resumed, "that since I started keeping to myself more, I don't hear from anyone unless it's business-related. I live here in this big house, so much room for me—and Cheryl, since I have her around these days. Did you know I'm forty years old?"

"Well," Bryce said, "I do now." His mouth felt dry. He raised his ginger ale for a drink.

"And I'm venting," Tabby said. "Sorry."

"I don't mind listening. I'm not always much of a talker."

"It all works out somehow, doesn't it?" She stood up. "Do you like music much?"

"Sometimes."

"Classical?"

"Not really."

"Blues?"

"I don't think I've listened to much of it."

"Come on," she said, and took his hand, surprising him. He allowed her to lead him out of the room, around the bend to the living room where Cheryl lay on one of the sofas, already asleep.

Tabby led Bryce to the record player. She crouched beside it to open a large, square black drawer Bryce hadn't previously seen, one of three containing an assortment of vinyl albums.

She slid an album out, removed the record from its sleeve, and handed the sleeve to Bryce. As she set the record turning, Bryce examined the album cover. On the background of a gray brick wall, it depicted a dark, heavyset man, bald, with an ebony guitar. He gazed outward, toward the left, his jaw clenched and his eyes focused.

The artwork was simple: the man and his guitar.

Beaumont Smiley, Broken Road Blues.

The strumming of Beaumont Smiley's guitar rose from the record player, the vocals quiet at first before driving into a deep rasp when the drums kicked in. The guitar's notes solidified, rising and slowly descending. Bryce continued to study the album's sleeve while he absorbed the music. Tabby had him curious.

"I met him once," Tabby said. "He used to play down by Candle Square sometimes. I don't think his music sat quite the right way with a lot of people around here back then."

"How's that?"

"Something about the vibe of it. It didn't make people happy, you see, and I think some people didn't understand its soul. He wasn't doing well health-wise or money-wise, I remember. I offered to buy him dinner, but he declined. I went to down to the bakery and brought him a bag of chocolate-chip cookies on my way back. He seemed to appreciate it.

"So many people don't realize how quickly they could lose everything and don't recognize what they have until it's out of their hands and it's too late. Because of where he was in his life in those days, I think Beaumont Smiley had a good understanding of that.

"After the Quake of '79, they say he moved on, some say back down to Louisiana where he was from, but I wonder, because it almost felt to me as if the quake had swallowed him up."

III

The phone rang. It was a white phone positioned inside the arch-doorway of the dining area. Tabby lowered the music and went to answer it.

"Hello, this is Tabby Reinhart," she answered. "Yes, he's here. Could you hold on for a minute?" She covered the mouthpiece. "Bryce?"

"What is it?" he replied. He left his place near the record-player and reentered the dining area.

"It's Paloma," Tabby said. "She asked about you. I told her you're still here. I'm not going to kick you out on your own if you don't have anywhere to go. I should be able to set you up with a temporary place for now, but we'll have to talk more later, after I look over your application. I have a few things to take care of today. I should get started on that. Do you mind catching a ride back with Paloma?"

"That's fine."

She returned to the phone. "Can you come out to give him a ride? Good. Back to 2803, for now. #4 is still empty. He'll be here waiting for you." She hesitated. "One more thing. Has George Loveless been around there since this morning's incident? I see. Thank you. Bye."

Looking at Bryce, Tabby hung up the phone. "Will that work? You'll be staying in #4 over by Paloma and Wheels."

"Sure," Bryce said, "but what about Loveless? What if he comes back?"

"Paloma said he hasn't been back out there yet, but given his behavior, I wouldn't rule anything out. Lock the door and the windows. Excuse me for a second." She moved past him into the living room, where she shook Cheryl gently by the shoulder.

Cheryl started and sat upright. "Sorry I fell asleep," she muttered. "Must have been the whiskey."

"That's all right. Do we still have those sleeping bags in storage?"

"I think so," Cheryl said. "I'll go look."

She climbed up and left the room. She returned sometime later with a red rolled-up sleeping bag, which she handed to Tabby. Tabby passed it to Bryce.

"I'm setting him up with a temporary living space," she explained to Cheryl, "until we can get a plan in place." She passed the sleeping bag on to Bryce. "It's unfurnished. I thought you would prefer this to sleeping on the carpet."

"Thanks," he said, and tucked it under one arm.

The record, its volume turned low, came to a stop.

"I'll have to make some phone calls since George isn't with us anymore," Tabby said. "I should get to it before it gets much later. Bryce, I have to say, it was really nice meeting you today."

"It was good meeting you, too," he said.

Tabby went to make her phone calls. Bryce stepped outside. The brightness of earlier had subsided. Afternoon now wore into early evening. He sat on the steps with the rolled sleeping bag in his lap and watched the gate.

In time, Paloma's tiny brown car pulled up to the gate. Bryce considered going to notify Tabby or Cheryl, but Cheryl came outside and accompanied him to the gate. She unlocked it, removed the chain, and opened the gate.

Anybody Want to Play WAR?

"Good meeting you," Cheryl said, and relocked the gate once he was through. Without a moment's delay, she headed back toward the house.

Paloma sat back in her seat with her hands on top of the steering wheel until Bryce climbed in. She shifted the car into reverse, looked back and around, and backed onto the street. She pushed the car into gear and drove away.

They turned through the streets of east downtown St. Charles. Paloma didn't speak until they reached Hatch Street and made their route west past Candle Square.

Here, she said, "You're a bad liar. Has anyone else ever told you that?"

"What did I do?" Bryce replied, taken by surprise. What did she think he was lying about this time? He hadn't said anything since getting into the car!

"What do you think you're trying to do?" Paloma asked.

"Nothing. What are you talking about?"

"If there is something I need to know, you should tell me. And you had better not try to drag Tabby into some kind of mess. I'm saying this now, between the two of us, because I know you aren't what you say you are. What did you tell her?"

"Why am I under fire here?" Bryce retorted. "What the hell did I do?"

"You realize all of this with Loveless is because of you, don't you?" Paloma said. "If he comes around trying to cause problems for the rest of us—"

"I'll take the heat for it," Bryce said. "Fine. Shit. If I'm such a problem for you and everybody else, why don't you just drop me off right here?"

"I told Tabby I would give you a ride back. I'll drop you off when we get there."

Bryce didn't say anything else. Paloma was agitated. Bryce was pissed.

Paloma was right, he knew, even if he would never admit it to her, and that pissed him off even more.

Finn

I

The instant Paloma pulled into a parking slot, Bryce jumped out of the car and launched up the stairs to the empty apartment. He unrolled his sleeping bag on the floor, laid down on it, and stared at the ceiling.

In truth, he didn't know much about Paloma, did he? But it was almost like she could look at him and read his mind, and she had pretty much told him he was nothing but a piece of shit.

Coming from her, it might be true. That was the worst part of it.

Except for Loveless showing up, things had been good at Tabby's, almost too good. He should have known it wouldn't last.

At least he had a place to stay for now, thanks to Tabby. He hoped he wouldn't wake up with George Loveless kicking the shit out of him again.

He got up to check the window. It was locked. He double-checked the door, and all was secure.

He sat back down on the sleeping bag. It wasn't long before he laid down again, but his mind raced. It was too early for sleep, he judged after several restless minutes.

Bryce limbed to his feet and, wondering if he had any money left, reached into his pocket to find a couple of dollars, some quarters, and a dime.

Sundown drew near, but he had another hour or so until everything went dark. He walked out to the street and followed it along its shoulder, back toward the Laundromat. He might get in a game of Asteroids while he was there.

He also remembered the pay phone in the corner of the Laundromat. Maybe he would call Finn. He wanted to talk to someone, a rare occurrence these days. His thoughts returned to that incident at school. He wondered about what had happened since he had left his house, and how it had gone at school after his suspension.

To his annoyance, the Laundromat was much busier than before. The parking lot was full. People crowded the small building's interior, busy customers rushing to do their laundry, kids shouting, and parents snapping irritably at them. Two children occupied the Asteroids machine. An older man wearing a brown-and-yellow trucker hat jabbered on the corner pay phone.

"No, you don't understand!" the man protested into the phone. "That's what I'm saying! I didn't say that! No. We're done, you hear me?"

The man's arguing blended with the rest of the noise in the Laundromat, threatening to give Bryce a headache. To his relief, the man finally slammed the phone down and stormed out. This gave Bryce an open route to the phone. He shoved between a hefty gray-haired woman and a younger dark-haired mother of three to grab the phone. He fished in his pocket for a coin and made the call.

Someone answered it on the first ring. "Hello?" It wasn't Finn. It was Mr. Finn, his dad.

"Hello," Bryce said. "Is Finn—Patrick—there?"

He hoped the man wouldn't ask, *who is this?* He would have to tell another lie. Even worse, what if Mr. Finn recognized Bryce's voice?

"Hold on," Mr. Finn said. Bryce leaned against the phone.

"Hello?" Finn answered.

"Finn, it's me. Bryce."

"What? Where are you?"

"What makes you think I'm not at home?"

"Somebody said they saw the cops at your house. I called over there, but you weren't home. Your mom was freaking out. She said nobody could find you. Then your dad got on the phone and started asking me a bunch of questions."

"He isn't my dad. He's my step-dad."

"You know what I mean. Where are you?"

This was the second time Finn had asked. Bryce bypassed the question.

"What else is going on?" he asked. "Have people have been talking about me at school?"

"They were yesterday, for sure."

"What were they saying?" Bryce asked. Before Finn could begin, he interjected, "You know what? Don't even bother telling me. It's about time I stopped giving a damn what any of those people think."

"I don't know, man. What about Brittany?"

"Brittany who?"

"Brittany Price. Remember her? You used to have a thing for her, didn't you?"

"When did I ever say that? But yeah, I remember her, even though right now I couldn't care less."

The only image of Brittany in his mind was the one of her laughing at him as Nate ran his mouth in the school hallway. Her giggling had stopped the moment he punched Nate to the floor.

"Hello?" Finn spoke.

"I'm still here," Bryce said. "But I should go."

"Got it," Finn said. "But can I ask you one more question?"

"What?"

"What the hell are you *doing*?"

"Good question. You know, Finn, I think I'm just tired of

all the bullshit. Later, man."

He hung up the phone and looked back over to the Asteroids machine. Those same kids were still playing it. He didn't feel like waiting around all night. The crowded Laundromat made him anxious, so he left.

II

Back at the apartment building, Bryce climbed the stairs to his temporary apartment and opened its door. He hesitated before switching on the light. A thought scurried through his mind, or it might have been a touch of paranoia, that George Loveless could be waiting inside to beat him to a bloody heap.

He made a quick search through every room, including the closet, to make sure that wasn't the case. Once satisfied he was alone, Bryce locked the door and ensured the window was still locked as well.

Lying down on the sleeping bag, he stared at the wall with its tiny bumps beneath a layer of cheap white paint.

He shouldn't have called Finn. Now it made him think of the things he had left behind, things that, if they ever caught up with him, could bring a hail of consequences down on him.

He wished he had a cigarette. A memory drifted through his mind, one of hiding out and smoking a cigarette with Finn at school, complaining, "Man, I sure do hate this school."

Finn had echoed the sentiment. They didn't agree on everything, but they agreed on that.

"I don't know what's worse," Bryce had said, "coming to school or going home. I can't stand it anywhere anymore. I've got to get out of this place." He waved his cigarette all around and at the back wall of the school library.

"Do your work like a good nerd and maybe you'll graduate," Finn said.

"And have to stand up in front of everybody and wear one of those stupid-looking graduation caps? No way. But I don't just mean getting out of this school, I mean getting out of St. Charles altogether. Getting on out of here and never looking back."

"Oh yeah? Where would you go?"

"Somewhere else."

"You haven't thought about that part yet, have you?"

"I got plenty of time to think about it."

"LA is where the party is."

"Maybe," Bryce said. "Or New York."

"You don't want to go to New York," Finn said. "You'll get yourself stabbed up there."

The bell rang. Bryce snubbed his cigarette against the brown back wall of the library building. Finn took a last drag before snuffing his own out and throwing it aside. They hurried to class.

The memory swirled down into slumber.

The Job

Bryce stirred in a sleepy fog of peaceful silence until a knock at the door roused him.

He gathered himself up, crept to the curtained window, and pushed the curtain aside to peer out. It was dark and early. He saw Wheels standing near the door, so he unlocked and opened it.

"Time to get started," Wheels said.

"What are you talking about?"

"Time to go to work. I'm supposed to show you the ropes today. You drink coffee?"

"No."

"You might want to start. We got a long day ahead of us."

Bryce yawned and brushed a hand through his hair. He came outside and closed up the apartment. With a quick motion, Wheels used a small iron key to lock the door.

"Oh, you have a key?" Bryce asked.

"Yeah. Here." Wheels handed over the key and started down the stairs. Bryce pocketed the key and followed him.

Wheels rounded the base of the stairway and fired up a cigarette. After an initial slow drag, he removed the cigarette from his mouth and leaned against the railing.

"What you'll be doing today isn't too hard," he said. "The grass needs mowing, so you'll be taking care of that. I'll need you to pick up some trash, too. I'm leaving a list with you because I've got a few things lined up for the day myself."

"You're leaving?"

"Yeah, eventually. I have more than just this building to keep up with."

"How do you get around with no car? Does Paloma drive you everywhere?"

"I have a bike. I got it for twenty dollars at a garage sale, but it works. It gets me where I need to go, around this part of town. I wouldn't ride my bike all the way out to Tabby's, though. That would be like riding through the seventh circle of Hell. You don't have a driver's license, do you?"

"Not yet."

"How old did you say you were again?"

"Eighteen."

With another puff of his cigarette, Wheels went silent. Fearing Wheels detected his lie this time, Bryce broke the silence with a distraction.

"Can I get a cigarette?"

"Another one? Damn." Wheels flipped one out and handed it over, along with a pack of matches. Bryce struck a match to light up his own cigarette.

He took in a deep smoke. "Thanks," he muttered, passing the matches back.

"About time you started buying your own."

"I would if I had money."

"Get your work done today and we'll see if we can't fix that."

They smoked their cigarettes. Wheels put his out on the ground. Bryce did the same. Without knowing why, he drew Wheels's glare.

"What's first?" Bryce asked.

"You can start by picking up that cigarette butt. When

you've picked up enough of those things, you'll know not to throw your trash on the ground for other people to worry about."

Bryce did indeed pick up a lot of cigarette butts within the next hour as the sun rose, as well as paper and a couple of discarded bottles. At some point, as Bryce walked around picking up trash at Wheels's instructions, Wheels disappeared. He returned with a dusty red push lawnmower and a red gas can.

"Where did you find that thing?" Bryce asked.

"Tool shed."

"Where's the tool shed? I didn't see any shed around here."

"It's around back." Wheels set down the gas can, uncapped the mower, and checked the tank. "You should have enough gas to finish this around here. Do the front and back. Here's a dollar. Go fill the gas can up when you're done. You can handle this, right?"

"Shouldn't be a problem."

"Good. When you're done, put it all back in the tool shed. Just take a good look around back. It's back there, trust me. You'll need this." He tossed another key to Bryce, this one a bronze key. Bryce caught it.

"I'll catch you later," Wheels said. He vanished behind the apartment building and came back around pushing a bicycle. He hopped onto it and took off with an upward-nod as he passed, heading for Hatch Street, where he made a right-turn onto the shoulder.

Bryce yanked the lawnmower's pull cord. A disgruntled sputter died in the mower. He tried again. After three pulls, the motor started with a shaky rumbling.

He pushed the lawnmower, cutting a row across the front, but had to go over the row again to ensure an even cut. He had to do this multiple times throughout the process of cutting the lawn's front portion. The inefficiency persisted when he moved along the edge of the lot to cut the still-dewy left side.

He discovered a few rocks strewn across the lawn. The lawnmower's blade banged one and whacked it against the side of the building. It bounced away, fortunately striking no windows. Afterward, Bryce exercised more care in scanning the grass for rocks.

By the time he reached the right side, the cutting became easier, but he missed another rock hidden in the grass. With a loud bang, it struck the side of the apartment building.

When he finished, he let the lawnmower's motor die and dragged the mower around to the back. He spotted a gray-painted door in a small rear protruding section of the building this time. He hadn't noticed it before but assumed this to be the tool shed Wheels had mentioned. It resembled more of a storage closet than an actual shed.

He tried the last key Wheels had given him and it worked. The door opened into a musty storage room crammed with tools and containers. He heaved the mower in and retrieved the gas can. He shook it. It was empty. At least he wouldn't have to carry it all the way down to Tuck's, because there was a closer gas station-garage up the street in the other direction.

II

Bryce barely had enough change in his pocket to grab a soda from the gas station's cooler. He stopped for a few minutes to drink it down and slung the glass bottle into a trash can by the gas station's front door. The caffeine and sugar helped somewhat in bolstering his steps as he lugged the newly filled gas can back to the apartments.

He saw Paloma's little brown car parked in the lot. He carried the gas can around to the tool room to lock it up. When he returned to the front lot, Paloma stood outside waiting for him.

"Wheels called," she said. "He needs you to help him over at 5808. I can give you a ride."

Anybody Want to Play WAR?

"Don't you ever get tired of driving people around?" Bryce asked.

"Wheels is a friend," she said once they climbed into the car. "He's been there for me and has given me money for gas several times. Besides, if I wasn't able to do it, I would say so."

She started the engine, backed out, and took a right onto Hatch Street. Bryce remembered the words they had fired at each other the day before, but he wasn't angry anymore, and she didn't seem to be, either.

When she had said he was lying about who he was, it was the truth, but how was he supposed to fix it now? The damage was already done, if any damage *was* done. Going back on what he had said would only make things worse, and he wasn't in any hurry to go back to a life where every day was shit.

So now he had a job. It wasn't great, but it was probably better than nothing. Wheels had trusted him to get the job done, and he had done it. Somehow that made him feel better, but the day wasn't over.

Out of boredom, he opened the glove compartment. He saw a pen, some papers folded in three, and a deck of cards inside. He reached for the cards.

"Looking for something?" Paloma asked. Bryce halted, caught in an instant of thoughtless prying, but then went ahead and took out the cards.

The card case was of golden-brown paper, decorated with pictures of small black diamonds and a black fleur-de-lis in the center. He opened the case and slid out a card.

"You play?" Bryce asked. He flipped over the card. It was the jack of hearts.

"Play?" Paloma echoed. "Whatever do you mean?"

"Nothing. Never mind." Bryce returned the card to the deck and closed the case. He tossed the cards back into the glove compartment and snapped it shut.

Paloma paused, her gaze clinging to the road, before deciding to give him a real answer. "Poker," she said. "That was my game. No, I don't play much anymore."

"Gamble much?"

"What would give you that idea?"

"Something about the way you said it."

"You would be right. I used to be a bit of a gambler. Some even called me Lady Luck." While she kept her eyes on the road, she was in clear thought now.

"But luck had little enough to do with my game," she said. "It's more a matter of knowing the game, knowing the players, and knowing when to hold or fold." She straightened in her seat. "We're almost there. Just ahead."

They turned into another parking lot, a wider one in front of three side-by-side tan apartment buildings. Paloma found a space among the other parked cars and killed the engine.

Once they were out of the car, Paloma motioned to one of the upper-level apartments. "He's up there."

They made it almost halfway to the indicated apartment before its door opened and Wheels stepped out. He stopped to wipe his hands with a red grease rag and saw them from the upper-level railing.

"There's some grass around here that needs cutting, too," he called down to Bryce.

"We didn't bring the lawnmower," Bryce said.

"Don't need to," Wheels called. "We got another one out here. There's a whole other tool shed down here."

"You mean a tool room?"

"I know what I mean. Give me a minute and I'll come down and show you."

As it turned out, this one was an actual shed. It stood across the parking lot, a separate small maroon structure in a corner past the last of the apartment buildings.

Once Wheels met them below to point it out, Paloma looked toward her car. "If you don't need anything else..."

"No, we're good," Wheels said. "Thanks for bringing him over."

Paloma left them. Wheels led Bryce to the tool shed, where racks of tools, a lawnmower, and a red metal gas can waited.

"You know what to do," Wheels said.

III

Bryce cut the grass around the perimeter of the apartment complex. When he finished, he pushed the lawnmower back into the tool shed and went to cleaning up trash as he had done at the other location. Wheels came outside, saw him working, and went back in to resume his project.

Later, Wheels wandered by and said, "Break time, little man."

"Why do you have to call me that?"

"Sorry." Wheels kept walking.

Bryce sat on the ground by the tool shed. Wheels came by a short time later with a brown paper bag in his hand.

"You bring anything for lunch?" he asked.

"Not a thing."

Wheels opened the brown bag and threw a bag of potato chips at Bryce. He reached to the bottom of the sack and brought out a mustard-smeared bologna sandwich. As Wheels leaned against the tool shed to eat his sandwich, Bryce popped open the bag of chips.

"How's the job?" Wheels asked between bites.

"It's work."

"I'll find more for you to do later, when I have time. You're just getting started today."

When Wheels finished his sandwich, he opened the tool shed door again and waved Bryce over. In the middle of a mouthful of crunchy potato chips, Bryce approached the shed's door, where Wheels pointed to the green weed eater hanging from a hook on the left wall.

"You got the weed eating done at the other place, right?" Wheels asked.

"No. You didn't say anything about it."

"We'll worry about that later. You can do it around here, though, right? You know how to use one of these?"

"Yeah." He had helped his mother and Richard with the weed eating around the house on a few occasions.

"Good," Wheels said. "Then you know what to do."

After that, Wheels disappeared again. Once Bryce finished eating, he went back to work.

Into the afternoon, Wheels stood outside wiping his hands with a rag again. He checked his watch.

"Almost time to call it a day," he said. "Let's lock it up."

Bryce pushed back his sweat-dampened hair. He realized he hadn't changed clothes in a while and guessed he probably smelled like shit, even if Wheels didn't say anything about it.

After replacing the padlock on the tool shed door, Wheels retrieved his bicycle, which he had stashed behind the shed.

"She should be around any time," he said with another glance at his watch. As predicted, it wasn't long before Paloma's small brown car pulled into the lot.

Wheels climbed onto his bicycle. "Thanks for the help today," he said. "It's good to see you don't mind doing a day's work. Catch you later."

He took off on the bicycle. Sweaty and tired, Bryce walked to Paloma's car and climbed in.

"I wish I had some clothes to change into," he said.

"You don't have any other clothes?" she asked.

"This is it. No money, either."

Paloma looked at him for a long time, making him uncomfortable, but she finally said, "Tabby might give you a day's advance if you ask her. I can take you by there if you want."

"Sure," he said. "That would be good."

She drove from the lot and turned right onto the street. After a quiet ride and a couple of additional turns, Paloma slowed near a small white building and pulled in its front lot.

Anybody Want to Play WAR?

Haven Properties, the sign read in red letters against a white background.

"This used to be Loveless's office, but Tabby should be here today," Paloma said. "That's her car. I'm sure she's filling in until she can find a replacement for Loveless. I'll wait here."

The white Corvette parked beside the building immediately drew Bryce's attention. *Now that's the kind of car I want to drive someday,* he thought.

He walked past it toward the building's glass front door. He grasped the handle to open it, but the door was locked. He tapped on the door.

He discerned a vague movement beyond the glass door. A click sounded. The door opened a portion.

"Come in," Tabby said.

As soon as Bryce stepped inside, the phone rang. Tabby hurried to a mahogany desk adorned with a desk lamp, a folder and pens, and a black telephone. She answered the phone and launched into what sounded like a business call, so Bryce waited and continued to look around.

A beige filing cabinet stood to one side of the desk and against the wall. The office had windows, but all were covered with white Venetian blinds.

When Tabby finished the phone call, she said to Bryce, "Sorry. How was your first day with Wheels?"

"It was okay."

"I'm sure he appreciates the help. I talked to him on the phone earlier."

"What did he say?"

"We didn't speak for long, but he did say it was coming along well."

"Is there any way I can get an advance for today's work? I don't have much money."

"I can do that. Hold on."

She opened a drawer, removed a black money pouch, unzipped it, and counted out two bills. She handed two twenties over. Bryce folded the crisp twenty-dollar bills together and slipped them into his left front pocket.

"Thanks," he said.

"You're welcome. Anything else?"

"I guess that's it. How's it going for you today?"

"It's—I don't know. I'm getting by."

"Is anything wrong?"

"It's nothing I can't deal with." She paused, but soon selected another subject. "While you're here, I should ask, did you happen to bring your ID with you this time?"

Bryce checked his pockets, though he knew he didn't have any such thing.

"Not this time," he said.

"Bring it when you have a chance, will you? I need to make a copy of your information."

The phone rang. Tabby cast a tentative glance at it.

"I have to take this," she said. "Sorry. I've been busy today."

"It's okay. Paloma is waiting for me outside."

"I'll see you later, then," Tabby said. "Have a good day, all right?"

"Thanks. I'll try. Same to you."

Bryce went back outside and got into the car. Paloma idly watched the side of the building with a hand on the steering wheel. When Bryce shut the car's door, she restarted the engine and shifted the car into reverse.

"Back to the apartment?" Paloma asked.

"I've been thinking I need to get some new clothes," Bryce said. "Could you drive me by somewhere?"

Paloma nodded, eased the vehicle across the small lot, and swung the car onto the street.

Foolish Notions

I

After his shower, Bryce reached for a towel only to realize he hadn't bought any. He toweled off with one of his new shirts instead. At least he had remembered to buy some soap and shampoo from the store, along with a few other basic items including a couple of cheap sets of clothes.

It irked him that he still wasn't old enough to legally smoke. Less than an hour ago, he had money in his pocket and his eyes on a wall of cigarettes behind a store counter. The clerk, a lanky woman with glasses and a pointy nose, had resembled a bird to Bryce. She stared at him with thick suspicion as she rang up his purchase. He didn't dare to ask her for a pack of cigarettes. He got a pack of peppermint gum instead.

After drying himself, he popped a stick of the gum into his mouth and threw on some clothes, jeans and a black short-sleeve shirt. He pulled on some clean white socks and shoved his feet back into his sneakers, which were white with faint smears of grass-green along the sides. After tying his shoes, he went outside.

Stars glittered from a blue-and-black sky. Bryce smelled cigarette smoke.

He went downstairs. On the other side of the building,

behind the railing in front of the upper apartment, he spotted a cigarette's red burning tip.

"Hey, Wheels," Bryce called.

"Yeah."

"Can I get a smoke?"

"How did I know that was going to come out your mouth?"

Bryce made his way up the other stairs. Wheels handed him a cigarette and a book of matches once he reached the top, but said, "You need to start buying your own damned cigarettes."

Bryce dug into his pocket and withdrew a rumpled dollar. "Here, this is for another pack of cigarettes."

Wheels took it.

"We're good now, right?" Bryce asked.

"Yeah, I guess."

He flipped open the matchbook, struck a light, and lit his cigarette. He drew in the smoke and gazed across the dark parking lot. Paloma's car was absent.

"Where's Paloma?" Bryce asked.

Wheels took a drag and released it upward. "She went to work."

"This late? What does she do?"

"She works at Pep's down at Candle Square, serving up thirsty crowds most nights."

For a while, they smoked without further conversation until Bryce remarked, "I saw Tabby today at the office."

Wheels didn't respond.

"She said she'd been busy today," Bryce added.

Wheels extinguished his cigarette against the rail. A trace of fiery ash spun downward into the dark.

"She kind of acted like something was wrong," Bryce continued, "but she wouldn't really say. I was thinking I should call and check on her. Do you have her number?"

"It'll be fine," Wheels said. "It's just stress. She had to take over for Loveless, remember? She's busy."

"Maybe that's all it is," Bryce said. "But I thought I should call her and make sure she's all right, and say thanks for giving me the job here and a place to stay until I can get things worked out."

"I don't think you're gonna be helping anything by doing all that."

"Why?"

"Listen." Wheels placed his hands on the rail. "Tabby does her thing and we do ours. We don't call over there and bother her unless we have a good reason, like what happened with Loveless."

Bryce removed the cigarette from his mouth. "You're saying I shouldn't talk to her?"

"I'm telling you, don't get any foolish notions in that head of yours. Now, we got another day of work tomorrow, and I think we should call it a night and get some rest, all right?"

"I guess so."

"Good night." Wheels turned from the railing, went into his apartment, and closed the door.

Bryce smoked his cigarette down and considered the words Wheels had dropped on him. He wasn't sure he got it. Did Wheels have a problem with him calling Tabby? If so, why?

He still held the pack of matches Wheels had given him, he realized. The matchbook was white with a plain black logo across the front, *The Lunchbox Café*, and a phone number beneath. Since he had the impression Wheels didn't want to be bothered anymore, Bryce shoved the matches into his pocket.

When he finished his cigarette, he walked downstairs to the lot, crossed to the street, and aimed his steps for the nearest place that might have a phone, that little gas station. It didn't take long to get there, but when he arrived, the lights were out.

This irritated him. Why did they close so early?

An alternative occurred to him, the Laundromat. He began walking that way.

II

The Laundromat was open, and there weren't many people here this time. No one occupied the Asteroids machine, but Bryce ignored it this time. Instead, he asked the lady behind the counter-and-window what time it was.

"I think it's a quarter after," she said.

"A quarter after what?"

She stared at him. "Nine."

Bryce didn't see why the people wouldn't put up a clock in here. When the woman saw he wasn't going away, she asked, "Is there anything else I can help you with?"

"Do you have a phone book here?"

She retrieved one from an unseen location behind the window and passed it through. Bryce flopped it open, turned to the *R*'s, and searched for Tabby Reinhart's number. He couldn't find it listed.

He closed the phone book and handed it back. "Do you have change?" he asked, pulling out a couple of loose dollars.

The woman made change for it without speaking. He scooped up the change, dumped it into his pocket, and walked to the pay phone. He snatched the phone from its cradle and dialed the number for information.

"Tabby Reinhart," he told the operator. "In St. Charles." When the operator asked how to spell the name, Bryce cautiously spelled it out. A period of silence made him wonder if he had gotten it right, but then she rewarded him with the number.

He searched around for a pen or pencil and some paper, anything to write with or on, but found nothing. He hung up the phone and quietly recited the number to himself. He dropped a coin into the slot, dialed the number on his lips, and placed the phone to his ear.

"Hello? This is Tabby Reinhart."

"Tabby, this is Bryce. Is everything all right?"

"Yes, I'm just sitting here at home. Did you need

something?"

"Not really. I thought I would call and check on you. When I saw you earlier, you seemed—well, I'm not sure."

Tabby didn't immediately reply. Discomfort trickled into Bryce. He questioned whether he had overstepped his bounds in calling.

"Things aren't perfect," Tabby said, "but I told you I could deal with it."

"What's wrong?"

"George Loveless called me at the office today, several times, harassing me and making threats."

"What? Are you serious? Fuck him."

"I told you not to worry about it," Tabby said. "I'm telling you because you asked. It's my problem, not yours."

"Maybe somebody should do something about him."

"Somebody like who? You?"

"That's right. Somebody exactly like me."

"Really?" Tabby sounded amused. "What would you do?"

"There's nothing he can do to you or me that I can't do to him five times worse. If he wants a war, I can give it to him."

"You think you're that much of a monster, do you?"

"I could be."

She paused, as if considering his words. "No," she said. "Let me handle it. I can have the police on him if it comes down to that."

Bryce yielded. This was her decision, he would give her that, even if he still felt he owed Loveless a little something for their scuffle that first day.

"All right," Bryce said. "But if you need anything, let me know."

Another question entered his mind. He almost hesitated to ask, but before Tabby could speak again, he gave voice to it.

"Do you want me to come by?" he asked.

"Over here?" Tabby asked, a pointless question, but her tone held a note of surprise. "It's up to you. There isn't much happening around here."

Bryce wasn't sure how to interpret this. "Do you want me to?"

Tabby deliberated. "I wouldn't mind the company," she said. "But I hope you don't expect much. I'm just sitting here with a martini, listening to music. It's been a long day."

III

What had he gotten himself into? How was he supposed to get all the way to Tabby's in the heart of downtown St. Charles? He wasn't about to walk, that was for sure.

Bryce pulled the keys from his pocket. He found the key to the tool shed, or the tool room as it actually was, and went around to its door in the back. He unlocked it and peered into the dark cluttered room to find the bicycle stashed to one side of the room.

If Wheels knew, he wouldn't be happy about it, so Bryce didn't ask him. He took the bicycle, locked up the tool room, and hopped onto the bike. He took off along Hatch Street, moving for east downtown.

He would try to have the bike back by morning, Bryce told himself. At least this was faster than walking. He pushed hard, pedaling fast and watching for obstacles.

In the back of his mind, he knew this was foolish. He had to admit to himself, although he hadn't said it out loud, that he liked Tabby more than was probably healthy.

These days, east downtown St. Charles wasn't the place to be on the streets alone at night. If you weren't especially lucky, bad things could happen there.

Lady Luck wasn't with Bryce today; she was busy serving up drinks in a little bar in Candle Square.

Sevens

I

Bryce pedaled eastbound on Hatch Street. His eyes remained on the street ahead until distant lights entered his vision.

Rows of white lights marked each sloped side of the reconstructed River Bridge. Down by the river, beyond the distance and blackness, a grassy strip yielded trees and homes across a curving valley.

The pale streetlights lessened ahead. Small houses lined this segment of darkened road, several in disrepair and some neglected entirely.

The road became bumpy. The front tire dipped into a pothole. The bicycle bounced and jerked. Bryce zigzagged and skidded to the shoulder to retain control.

After almost going into a ditch, he decided to slow down and exercise more caution. Without decent lighting, he couldn't see much around him. He kept to the shoulder until he saw the lights of Candle Square.

The lights appeared brighter as he rode nearer. A few dark forms crossed the street. Soon, the murmurings of voices cut through the crunching of the bicycle's tires over the roadside gravel. Bryce maneuvered to the road's right side and pedaled past the lots and clustered buildings of Candle Square.

A number of people milled around outside, many coming and going from the bars and nightclubs. He scanned the signs that were lit and readable. Which one was Pep's, where Paloma worked? By the time he passed all of them, he still had no idea.

He rode past Summerset Park, eerie in the faint yellow glow of its lamppost. Dark shrubs bordered the park. A floral scent touched the air.

Past the park, the lights diminished again. Some distance onward, he passed a narrow, unlit elm-bordered road on the left, Cemetery Road.

Feeling an odd apprehension, as if someone watched him, Bryce rode faster.

After a considerable distance, he slowed again to give his legs and feet a break. He coasted by a closed grocery store. Down the street, he observed another smattering of lights and a couple of neon signs. A flickering red sign indicated the King's Motel, behind which a man had been murdered for his lunch, spare cash, and a few cigarettes.

He didn't ride as far as the motel. Instead, he slowed beside a low-key burger joint to his right and made his turn. He thought this was the way. He did his best to recall the route from that uncomfortable ride in the back compartment of Paloma's car.

The lighting desisted again.

Things waited in the darkness, Bryce imagined, watching. He had sensed it as he passed the road to the cemetery but didn't know why. The feeling was like a cousin to the strange fear he remembered from his helpless youth.

Bryce was still young, but no longer helpless. If anything challenged him here, he would do his damnedest to defy it. This was more than he could have said for the child he was when his uncle gave him the pocketknife.

Now he rode through the dark heart of St. Charles, a place of shadows, unrest, and murder, and he didn't have his pocketknife, or any weapon at all.

Anybody Want to Play WAR?

Two shadows passed in his peripheral vision. Bryce whipped his head around to track the source of the movement but saw only the stagnant darkness. Had he imagined it? Were his fears getting the best of him again?

No, he told himself, because he hadn't turned back. Not yet.

Graffiti marked the walls of the buildings around him. Obscenities, death threats, sevens.

Why did Tabby live out here? Why didn't she live somewhere north of the river like the rest of those optimists of the American Dream who sipped their cocktails and dressed the part?

Because Tabby, Corvette and martinis aside, wasn't one of those people. There weren't many people like Tabby that Bryce knew of.

Another shadow distracted him. When he looked toward the slender alleyway, he saw nothing but a trash can until a figure stumbled across the road in front of him and forced him to swerve.

It was a skinny man with rumpled greasy hair and dirty clothes. A brown-bagged bottle dangled from his hand.

His course disrupted, Bryce stopped short of hitting the outside steps of a gray building. He braked to a rough stop, backed away, and intended to propel himself around the obstacle and forward again, but a sense of unease prompted a careful look around.

A leather-vested man with a mess of unkempt dark hair startled him. The young man watched from the opposite side of the stone steps. A toothpick protruded from his mouth.

He had observed Bryce's encounter with both the drunk and the steps. He reached up to remove the toothpick from his mouth with his thumb and forefinger.

"Nice bike," the man said with an amused, sarcastic tone. He raised his eyes to confront Bryce's. "What happened to your face?"

"Piss off," Bryce said. Right away, he didn't like this son-of-a-bitch.

"Don't get mad," the young man said. "I'm just making conversation. Can't you handle that?"

"You're an asshole."

"Call me what you want, but let me tell you, you need to watch out around here." He stuck the toothpick back in his mouth, crossed his arms, and slouched back against the wall.

"Why's that?"

The man surveyed Bryce. "I got a feeling you ain't going to have many friends out here. This place might not be safe for you, know what I mean? Maybe you should turn around and go back the way you came."

"Or else what?"

"I'm just giving you some friendly advice, that's all."

"Yeah, right." Bryce guided the bicycle around the steps in a wide curve. "Good luck handing out friendly advice to strangers tonight, like anybody gives a damn."

Bryce climbed back onto the bicycle and pushed away. He hadn't made it far before two dark-haired figures approached on the street.

The man in the leather vest laughed behind him. "Oh, shit," he said. "Here they come!"

Bryce braked to a stop. One of those walking toward him had a black bandana wrapped around his head. He wore a black tank top with a green number 7 painted onto it. The other, a shaggy-haired one whose faded jeans were torn in a few places, wore a black vest with a 7 painted across a vest pocket.

I don't have time for this, Bryce thought. He shifted his direction toward the left-branching street, but found his redirected route blocked by three more figures with black shirts, all marked with 7's.

"What you doing around here, boy?" one of the two blocking his original path asked. "You lost?" The other beside him didn't speak but reached to a compartment on his black vest to withdraw a knife.

"Where the fuck you think you are, princess?" another asked. "Disneyland?"

Bryce knew where he was now, though he hadn't been down this way aside from the times he had ridden in Paloma's car. This had to be 7th Street, and these were the 7th Street Sevens.

"Look at his face," one of them said. A few laughs followed. A familiar low boil of anger stirred in Bryce, but he couldn't ignore the fear diluting it.

"That ain't nothing compared to how it'll look when I'm finished," the man with the knife said.

Alone and unarmed, Bryce knew the odds were vastly against him. This wasn't some fight at school. It certainly wasn't Nate Plunkett. This was life or death.

The sudden headlights of an approaching vehicle shone from behind. Bryce lunged for the initiative. He launched forward on the bicycle and veered around the two in front of him, his best bet. He hurtled through and didn't look back.

He heard footsteps racing behind him. He rode fast along the roadside as the car, its headlights bright, sped by the Sevens and past him.

His vision flashed and pain stabbed through his back of his head. He latched onto a fire of self-preservation, anchored his hands to the handlebars, and pushed to maintain the numb, hard pedaling.

"Run, you fucking pussy!" someone screamed. "Run or we'll fucking kill you!"

They would try, he knew. They'd hit him with something, and it hurt, had almost knocked him out, but he couldn't waver now.

He saw another street branching to the left and cut a sharp turn. The bicycle wobbled, but he steadied it and shot down the street to make another turn around a corner to the right. Under the shadows of a dark building, he sped into an alleyway.

There he crashed and reeled into a chain-link fence. The

bicycle bounced backward and scraped across the ground. Through his daze, Bryce saw a post protruding from the ground. In his race through the dark, he hadn't seen it, but he had definitely hit it.

A roar assaulted his ears. A black dog lunged against the chain-link fence, barking and snapping.

Bryce scrambled to his feet, heart pounding. His head spun. He rushed away. The Sevens shouted through the dog's furious din.

Bryce's head throbbed and his hands and shoulders hurt, but none of it stopped him. He ran for it.

More shouts carried. Bryce ran alongside the fence to another street, where he crossed and darted into the nearest shadowy crevice he could find. He gasped to catch his breath but struggled to keep his breathing low for fear they would find him.

He heard the crash of the bicycle against a brick wall. The dog snarled and leaped against the fence. One of the Sevens kicked the fence.

"Shut the fuck up!" he screamed at the dog.

The Sevens slammed the bicycle against the wall of the building again, kicked it, and stomped it. A couple of the others came out to the street. One roamed toward Bryce's hiding spot. Bryce fought to keep his heavy panting down.

The other one stood in the street, looking from one end to the other. "I don't see him," he said. "Little pussy's still running, I bet."

The one near Bryce chuckled. He walked away, back across the street, and the other one, with the knife in his hand, joined him. They rejoined the others, who had reduced the bicycle to a piece of bent, battered metal and shredded tires.

"Come on," the one wearing the black bandana said. The Sevens surged back into the alleyway, past the post that had wrecked Bryce, and disappeared into the night. The implacable fenced dog barked on.

Anybody Want to Play WAR?

Anybody Want to Play WAR?

II

Bryce didn't know this area, but from the appearance and smell of the boarded-up, broken-down structures around him and piles of refuse littered around, it seemed like a real shithole. He had no idea of how to get to Tabby's from here.

He touched the back of his head. It wasn't wet with blood, at least. They had thrown something at him. A bottle, a wrench, or a chain. Who knew? It hurt.

The dog wouldn't stop barking. Despite that, he didn't hear voices anymore and hadn't seen any signs of the Sevens in a few minutes. He slinked from his hiding spot. When nothing happened aside from the dog's continued barking, he ran.

Between two buildings, an alley stretched toward another street. He rushed that way. At the alleyway's end and across the next street, he spotted a corner shop with a green-and-white awning. He glanced around before hurrying toward it.

S & B Pawn, read the sign on the glass door. He tried the door. It wouldn't budge. He kept hoping to find a phone he could use, but it didn't happen here.

He skirted the buildings to his left and maintained stealth and caution across the next couple of streets. He didn't see anyone else, but that didn't mean someone, or something, wasn't around.

He saw a phone booth on the corner of the bend ahead. A streetlight shone onto it from above. Bryce lingered, reluctant to approach. He didn't want to broadcast his presence here, but he needed a phone.

In his pocket he felt the matchbook Wheels had given him, along with a few jingling coins. He had the change to make a call. He would call Tabby. He didn't have her number, but he had called information for it before. He should be able to do that again, provided he could make it to the phone and complete the call.

113

He took a breath, clenched his fists, and charged across the street to the phone booth. Pushing inside it, he grabbed the telephone and dialed information. When the operator answered, he asked for Tabby Reinhart in St. Charles.

"Sir, I'm going to have to ask you to slow down," the operator said. Bryce cursed internally, but repeated himself, more slowly this time. The operator gave him the number. He repeated it to himself as he had done before, hung up, and dialed it. The phone rang once.

"This is Tabby Reinhart's residence," a voice answered, though it wasn't Tabby.

"Cheryl?" Bryce spoke. "Is Tabby there?"

"Who is this?" Cheryl asked.

"This is Bryce."

"Bryce Stafford?"

Bryce hesitated, remembering he had lied about his last name.

"That's right," he said. "I'm somewhere in downtown St. Charles. I was on my way over and the Sevens came after me. Things got serious."

There came a pause on Cheryl's end. "Where are you?" she asked.

Bryce searched around for a street sign, but without success. "I'm not sure," he said. "Earlier I came by this little pawn shop, *S & B Pawn*. I'm a couple of streets down from that, at the phone booth on the corner."

He heard murmuring in the background. After an uncomfortable delay, Cheryl came back to the phone.

"Don't move far," she said. "Tabby's had a couple of drinks, but I can drive. We're coming out there to get you."

"Good. Thanks. Hurry."

Bryce left the phone booth and ran across the street. He found a dark corner and waited there.

Minutes crawled beneath the silence.

Headlights emerged onto the street. Bryce almost rushed out but soon became glad he hadn't. The battered, heavy green car rounded the corner without slowing. In the driver's seat sat a figure wearing a black bandana.

Bryce shrank against the building walls. He ducked low until the vehicle vanished from sight.

A short time after, another vehicle's headlights became visible. A white Corvette emerged into view. When it slowed near the corner, Bryce ran to it.

The window lowered a fraction. "Get in," Cheryl said from behind the wheel.

Bryce didn't have to hear it twice. He ran around to the passenger's side door. Tabby was there. She moved over as much as possible for him to squeeze in beside her. He slammed the door and locked it. Cheryl sped away.

"What happened?" Tabby exclaimed.

"Didn't Cheryl tell you?" he asked.

"You're hurt," Tabby said. Pressed against him, she leaned closer to examine him. Her close scrutiny prompted him to turn his head away. He looked out the window.

"I'll live," he said.

"You might need to go to the hospital."

"I would rather not."

"That's up to you, but—"

"I'm fine."

"Then I'll leave you alone about it."

"It's okay, Tabby. I've just had a bad night. Thanks for picking me up."

Cheryl spoke up. "What are you doing out here, anyway? Don't you know it isn't safe around here?"

"I think I have an idea, yeah," Bryce replied.

Tabby

I

Cheryl drove the Corvette onto the estate, parked it in the garage, and returned to lock the gate in place while Tabby and Bryce went into the house.

"I'm glad you're all right," Tabby said to Bryce. "I was worried. How did you end up out there?"

"I was trying to get over to your house."

"On foot?"

"I was riding a bicycle."

"You shouldn't have done that."

She led him to one of the white sofas and urged him to sit. While he settled onto the sofa, she went to the dining area. Bryce heard the sound of ice clinking into a glass and liquid pouring. She returned with a ginger ale on ice and another martini for herself. She handed the ginger ale to Bryce and sat down beside him.

Cheryl came in through the front door. Before she could take a seat on the other couch, the phone rang. She sighed and moved to answer it.

"Thanks, Cheryl," Tabby said, and micro-sipped her martini.

"It's a nice change having the lights on in here," Bryce

commented.

"I thought, 'what's the point?'" Tabby replied. "You've seen me." She brought the martini up for another sip. "I shouldn't expect anything to stay the same, even if I'm not the person I used to be. What happened to me last year in that wreck—it didn't make things easier, but it isn't only that. I lost a friend on that day of the quake. I don't talk about it much."

Her eyes lowered to the surface of her drink. "But I'm still here, getting older whether I like it or not, even though I feel like I've lost a part of myself. Time seems so short, and other people expect so much from me. Even worse, they expect me to be something I'm not, and people don't really care to understand, do they? They want what they want. I feel so overwhelmed sometimes. I don't even want to get out of bed some days."

"It could be worse," Bryce said. "You could be like me."

As soon as it left his mouth, Bryce hated that he'd said it. It reminded him of something Richard would say.

Tabby responded with a slight shake of her head. Resigned, she slumped back into the sofa.

"No, she doesn't want to talk to you," Cheryl's voice declared from beyond the doorway.

Tabby sat up straight again, both hands balancing her martini. Bryce leaned forward.

"If anyone's a bitch around here, it's you," Cheryl said. "Don't call over here again." She smacked the phone onto its receiver and emerged from the arched doorway.

"Was that who I think it was?" Tabby asked.

"Loveless," Cheryl said. "He told me to put you on the phone. I told him you didn't want to talk to him, and he started screaming at me."

"He's still calling you?" Bryce asked.

"He calls at the office and he calls at the house now," Tabby said.

"Like I said," Bryce said, "if you want me to do something

about him, let me know. Not tonight, though. My head hurts."

"You took on the Sevens tonight," Tabby mused. "Who knows? You might really be able to do something. I'm tempted to consider it."

"This whole thing *is* kind of my fault," Bryce said.

Cheryl collapsed onto the other sofa. "I think it might have happened anyway, one way or the other. Loveless has always been angry—a little too angry."

"I wonder why?" Tabby asked.

"Who can say for sure?" Cheryl replied. "The guy's divorced, lives alone, didn't seem to have much of a life outside his job. Now his job's gone."

"I had to let him go," Tabby said. "The way he talked to me, and coming to my house, threatening me—"

"You're absolutely right, boss," Cheryl said. She pulled her knees together and leaned forward, her arms encircling her knees. "But my point is, the man's like a ticking bomb."

II

Cheryl lay curled up on the couch, asleep. Tabby placed a white blanket over her and moved on to attend to Bryce, who had finally consented to let her inspect his injuries.

She handed him two aspirin tablets. He swallowed them with a drink of ginger ale. Tabby examined the back of his head and touched the tender area. He flinched.

"Sorry," she said. "It looks like you have a spot back here. What happened to you?"

"I think they threw something at me."

"I'll get something for those scrapes," she said, and withdrew. Bryce had skinned his knees and cut his arms during the bicycle crash, a fact he hadn't realized until now.

Tabby returned with a white can of antiseptic spray. "Hold still," she said. She shook the can and sprayed the affected areas. It burned, but Bryce didn't complain.

She set the can on the coffee table. Before she could

make it back onto the sofa, the phone rang.

Bryce glanced at Cheryl. She remained asleep.

"Want me to answer it?" Bryce offered. Tabby was halfway there already but paused. She gestured toward the doorway and the ringing phone.

"Be my guest," she said.

Bryce stepped through the doorway, took the phone, and placed it to his ear. Silence lurked at the other end.

"I know who this is," Bryce said.

No answer but a sharp exhalation and a *click*.

Tabby stepped through the doorway into the darkened dining area. "What did he say?" she asked.

"Nothing," Bryce said. "But I'm sure it was him."

"He didn't say anything at all?"

"Nothing."

She looked to the darker curve of the dining area's far end, where it met the bar. She appeared troubled. When she looked to Bryce again, she said, "You can leave the phone off the hook if you want."

He left the phone dangling by its cord. They returned to the living area, where Bryce took a seat on the edge of the sofa again and Tabby visited the record player.

She sifted through the albums until she reached a decision and set one to play. Soft strains of classical music drifted into the room, the sound low to avoid waking Cheryl. Tabby returned to the sofa and retrieved her drink from the coffee table.

"Next time you want to come by," she said, "just call. That will save you a few rounds with the Black Shirt Bunch."

"The Sevens?"

"Yes, that's just my little name for them." She shrugged and took a drink.

"You don't take them that seriously."

"Not really, not until tonight."

"It's different when they're trying to kill you."

"I bet it is. I'm glad you can take care of yourself. What

do you think about the music?"

Bryce stopped to listen. "It's all right."

"You don't like it much, do you?"

"To tell you the truth, it seems kind of boring."

"It's light classical. It helps me to relax."

"I liked what we listened to the other day better."

"The other day as in yesterday?"

"It was, wasn't it? It feels like it's been longer than that."

Tabby stood, setting her drink down, and went to remove the record. She held up another album, Beaumont Smiley's *Broken Road Blues*.

"Was this it?" she asked.

"That's the one," Bryce said. Tabby set it to play and returned to the couch.

The music started, soft at first, then rising to thunder down into Beaumont Smiley's "Going Nowhere."

"I wasn't sure what to think about this the first time I heard it," Bryce said. "It was different."

"And now you've decided you like it?"

"It had me thinking. That other record you had on just now was more like background music. This is the kind of music that refuses to sit down in the background. At the same time, it doesn't pretend to be happy, but it isn't apologizing about that, either. Does this make any sense, what I'm saying?"

Tabby laughed. "I think I understand what you're saying."

"It's good that somebody does."

"Would you say you aren't happy, then?"

"On the average day, no, but things are better than they used to be."

"That's good, at least."

"In a way, I have you to thank for that," Bryce said.

Tabby finished her martini and set the glass on the coffee table.

"And riding through downtown like I did tonight," Bryce continued, his eyes traveling to her glass on the coffee table, "with the Sevens chasing after me and trying to kill me, it seemed like a crazy thing to do at the time, but now maybe it doesn't seem so crazy."

Tabby surveyed him, her brown eyes quizzical. "What do you mean?" she asked.

"Maybe it was worth it," he said, looking to her eyes, her wavy brown hair, to the bodice of her red dress, and again to her wondering eyes, "because I did it for you. I can't say what it is, exactly. Maybe it's everything about you. I keep thinking about you, and I keep thinking you aren't like anyone I've ever known."

Was he speaking nonsense? He didn't know how else to convey it, how much he thought about her, that she had him whether she knew it or not, and that there was only one place for him now, right here with her.

He leaned in. His lips met hers. He pressed into her, kissing her deeply. For an instant, he imagined, she kissed him back.

She withdrew, startled. They stared at each other until Tabby stood from the sofa and moved to the record player. She hovered in front of it for a long time, watching the record spin, saying nothing.

Bryce couldn't think of a word to say. His hands were damp, he realized, even pressed against the legs of his pants. He took a slow breath, directed his gaze to a wall, and waited for Tabby to speak.

Oblivious in the presence of a quiet tempest, Cheryl lay sleeping on the other sofa.

Tabby ventured to disrupt the silence. "I can't—" She stopped, shaking her head. "I'm forty years old. Don't you realize that?"

"It doesn't matter to me," Bryce said.

Her eyes heavy with doubt, Tabby watched the record spin.

"I like you, I do, but listen to me," she said. "It's something that just can't be. You have your whole life ahead of you, and you'll meet a lot of girls your own age—"

Anybody Want to Play WAR?

"I can't stand the girls at school," Bryce muttered. He sank into the couch. "I can't stand teenagers, even if I am one."

"School?" Tabby spoke, her tone assuming an abrupt odd turn. "Do you mean *high school?*"

Bryce faltered. He sat up and looked at her again. "No," he said.

Tabby stared at him with guarded eyes. "I think you should leave."

"Tabby—"

"Cheryl," Tabby called. She strode over to lay a hand on Cheryl's shoulder and nudge her awake. Cheryl sat up, glancing around and up at Tabby with a start.

"What is it?" Cheryl asked.

"Can you take Bryce home?"

"Home?"

"Back to the apartment, for now," Tabby said. Her gaze was impenetrable. Again, Bryce wasn't sure what to say. Maybe she was right, and he should leave before things became any worse.

He accompanied Cheryl out to the garage. Tabby didn't speak to him on his way out. Still sleepy, Cheryl yawned, opened the garage, and started the car.

She reached back to straighten her hair. "Things seem weird," she remarked. "Is everything all right?"

"Everything's just great," Bryce said.

Cheryl glanced over. "Did something happen?"

Bryce found himself at a loss. He shook his head. Telling Cheryl wasn't likely to make things better.

He had no one else to blame but himself. He couldn't imagine what might be going through Tabby's mind right now. He felt helpless.

Cheryl backed the car out of the garage and closed the garage door. She drove to the gate and climbed out to unlock it. After she opened the lock, removed the chain, and opened the gate, she backed the Corvette through.

Through her murk of sleepiness, Cheryl hadn't noticed the white car parked up the dark street. As they backed out, Bryce saw it. It struck him as familiar, but he couldn't remember from where or why.

When they stopped at the edge of the street, a large white figure rushed at the car's driver's side window. Cheryl jumped in her seat. Bryce's muscles tensed. A baseball bat exploded through the window and glass showered them. There was scarce time to react before George Loveless seized Cheryl through the window and dragged her outside, screaming.

Meltdown

Loveless hurled Cheryl to the ground and slammed the baseball bat into her knee. The bone crunched, breaking, and she howled in agony.

Bryce fumbled with the passenger door's handle. At last, the door came open. He ejected himself from the car.

On the other side, Cheryl tried to pull herself up, but Loveless struck her with the bat again, this time hard in the back. She sprawled face-down onto the side of the road.

Bryce ran around the vehicle. Loveless faced him with the bat raised and murder in his eyes.

He delivered a vicious swing and Bryce backpedaled to avoid it. Loveless followed in with another swipe. Bryce wasn't quick enough this time. The bat clipped the side of his arm near his shoulder. It stung like a nest of angry wasps.

Bryce stumbled back. Loveless jabbed the bat toward him. "Go on, run, but I'll catch you. I guarantee it. And when I do, I'll bash your skull in."

Cheryl wasn't moving. Bryce wanted to check on her, but he couldn't chance taking his eyes away from Loveless. The man would come at him the instant he let his guard down.

He just hoped Cheryl wasn't dead.

Loveless stood with the bat in his hands and positive hatred in his stare, waiting for Bryce to make his move.

Bryce wouldn't run. He couldn't leave Cheryl at this man's mercy. Not after everything he had done, the lies he had told, and the damage he had caused.

He would spring at Loveless, try to take the man down somehow. He braced himself and moved to action.

Loveless saw it in his eyes and stance, and his eyes lit with triumphant fury. His squeezed the bat with anticipation.

A scream and a sudden piercing light from the front of the house halted them. The door had opened, the front light was on, and Tabby ran toward them.

Seeing his opportunity, Bryce lunged. He collided with Loveless, but the man's huge frame didn't even budge.

With his free hand, Loveless seized Bryce by the side of his head and flung him to the ground. Bryce gasped with the impact. Loveless raised the bat for a savage downward swing.

"Stop!" Tabby screamed. She stood in the glaring light, the gun in her hands trained on Loveless.

"If you make another move," she said, "I will shoot."

Loveless's pasty face was white in the house's bright light. Sweat dampened the pits and front of his white collared shirt, a few buttons of which were undone.

"Do it," he said. "I got nothing to lose. But you got everything to lose, bitch. Go on, shoot me!"

Bryce rolled away from Loveless. The big man's attention was rooted to Tabby now. His eyes were wide, and his teeth showed.

"You think I can't defend myself?" Tabby asked. "That I can't defend my friends? Try me."

Loveless chuckled. He threw the bat aside. "You have it in you to look in a man's eyes and shoot him dead?" He held up his arms and walked toward her. "Prove it."

Tabby cocked the gun's hammer. Loveless continued toward her.

Other lights had come on along the road, beaming from

the house diagonal and another on the opposite side of it. Figures stood outside and watched the spectacle from their distance.

Bryce stood again. He saw Cheryl on the ground, battered black-and-blue. She didn't stir, but she still breathed.

He didn't delay another second in taking up the discarded baseball bat. He went after Loveless.

Loveless still walked toward Tabby, his full attention on her, when the rapid footsteps from behind distracted him. As he stopped and turned, Bryce swung the bat into his head. With a meaty crack, Loveless spun and dropped to his knees.

He gripped his head with both hands. He swayed, doubled over, and vomited onto the driveway pavement.

Tabby's eyes grew round. She held the gun steady but stepped back.

Loveless raised his face to the light. A string of pink vomit hung from his lip. Blood welled from the back of his head. He moaned.

Tabby came forward a few steps with the gun ready. With a swift glance at Bryce, she said, "Watch him." Bryce nodded. Tabby moved well around Loveless, tucked the gun away, and ran toward Cheryl.

"Oh, no," she breathed. "No." She crouched beside Cheryl and fought to stifle a soft cry.

Sirens screamed in the distance. Bryce clutched the bat and kept his eyes on Loveless. His heart pounded. The sirens came closer.

"Cheryl," Tabby whispered. "What did he do to you?" She raised her voice, crying out. "Someone, help us, please!"

The neighbors stood motionless in front of their homes, but it had become apparent enough someone had already called the police. The sirens were almost here.

Soon, the blue lights of three police vehicles whirled onto the street. A uniformed man leaped out of one of the cruisers.

"Stop where you are!" he shouted. To Bryce's surprise,

the officer leaned across the open door of his police cruiser to aim a gun in his direction. "Drop the weapon!"

Bryce released the baseball bat. It clattered to the driveway.

Guns drawn, the police moved in. One kicked the baseball bat away. He and another officer handcuffed Bryce.

"Tabby, tell them what happened!" Bryce said.

Tabby, holding near Cheryl, snapped from her haze and stood up. "Not him," she said to the police. She pointed toward Loveless. "Him, there on the ground. He attacked us—attacked them. His name is George Loveless."

She swung back to Cheryl. "We need an ambulance, *now.*"

II

The ambulance turned in, slow and careful in its movements to navigate between the police vehicles. One police officer pulled Tabby aside.

"Miss Reinhart," he said, "we'll need to ask you a few questions."

"I'll do what I can," Tabby said. She wrapped her arms around herself as if chilled, but the night was warm.

Watkins, the young officer's name plate read.

Officer Watkins proceeded to question her about the night's events. She could hardly focus. Some distance away, the medical personnel carried Cheryl on a stretcher to the back of the ambulance. Tabby's eyes threatened to well with tears. She turned her stare toward the ambulance's spinning red lights.

Another officer had Loveless handcuffed by one of the police vehicles. A medic came over to examine the bleeding back of his head.

"Miss Reinhart?" Officer Watkins spoke.

"I'm sorry," she said. She returned her attention to Officer Watkins, who stood watching her with a pad of paper and a pen in hand.

The ambulance doors closed. The vehicle lurched away.

Tabby desperately wanted to follow Cheryl to the hospital, Bryce knew, but for now, the police kept asking questions and she forced herself to answer them.

Two other officers approached Bryce. One of them, whose name was Rosenbaum, addressed him. "Bryce Gallo?"

"What is it?" Bryce answered. Officer Rosenbaum and the other officer exchanged glances.

"Do you realize you've been reported missing?" Rosenbaum asked.

"What?" he asked. "That can't be right." Despite his attempted nonchalance, Bryce's heart thudded.

"You'll need to come with us," Rosenbaum said. The other officer moved closer to Bryce while Rosenbaum made a path toward Tabby and Officer Watkins.

"Miss Reinhart, is it?" Officer Rosenbaum addressed. "Has Bryce Gallo been staying here in your home?"

Watkins glanced up from his notes. Tabby was puzzled. "Who?" she asked.

"Bryce Gallo." Officer Rosenbaum pointed. "The kid standing right there."

"His last name is Stafford, isn't it?"

"No, ma'am. That's Bryce Gallo. Do you realize you've been harboring a minor? One who has been reported missing?"

Tabby hesitated for some time.

"He's eighteen," she said. "That is legal adult age, the last time I checked."

"No, he's sixteen, and his parents have reported him missing. Your harboring him here is a criminal offense, do you understand that?"

"What?" Tabby exclaimed. Gripped with obvious uncertainty and apprehension, she looked toward Bryce.

"Am I under arrest?" she asked the police.

"You'll need to come with us to the station," Officer

Rosenbaum said. She looked to Bryce one last time, at an utter loss for words, before the officers escorted her toward a police vehicle, a different car from the one carrying Loveless.

Bryce could barely breathe. He gave no resistance as the nearest officer took him by the shoulders and maneuvered him toward the third of the police cruisers.

Gasoline

I

The image sliced into Bryce's thoughts like a burning blade: Tabby's eyes as she had looked at him, her stunned realization of his betrayal. He wished he could have told her the truth, but he had always been afraid, and now it was too late.

Cheryl was on her way to the hospital. Bryce could do nothing for her. Loveless had hit her without mercy. Bryce wanted to spit on the man's bleeding bald head.

Wheels would discover his bicycle missing in the morning. He would also find out, by some channel, what had happened to Tabby.

Bryce could only sit in the back of a police car and think about how fucked up everything was. He had fought to make a change in his life and now the cards were wrenched from his grasp and flung to the wind.

Paloma, Lady Luck as they once called her—she knew all about cards, didn't she? She had tried to warn him, but he hadn't listened, and the memory was a splash of gasoline across the helpless anger that burned in his every thought.

The police cruiser took the slight curve from Hatch Street onto Dartmoor and slowed for the turn onto Evelyn Drive. The officer leaned over to examine the houses on the right side. When he found the address, he parked in front of the house.

"Wait here," he said, as if Bryce could do anything else.

Bryce had already tried the cruiser's back car door and found it couldn't be opened. This was his first time riding in a police car.

The officer knocked at the front door. When the door opened, Richard stood there in a white short-sleeve shirt. Soon Bryce's mother joined him.

Bryce couldn't hear the exchange from his position, but he saw the reactions. Richard was still and silent. Elaine's eyes were wide, her hands pressed together in front of her. Both of them glanced repeatedly toward the police car.

The officer returned to the car, Elaine with him. Richard remained at the front door.

The police officer opened the cruiser's back door. Bryce climbed out. His mother threw her arms around him.

"Bryce," she gasped. She had been crying. "I—we didn't know what—why —"

Bryce released a heavy sigh. For the moment, he could retreat from the burning anger of moments ago.

"I'm sorry," Bryce said. "I just couldn't take it around here anymore."

"How could you just—just *take off* like that?" she asked between sobs.

"I'm sorry. I don't know what else to say."

She stepped back and stared at him. She had tears in her eyes, but her expression was uncomprehending.

"Is everything all right now?" the police officer asked.

Elaine gaped at her son as if confronting some stranger. Richard watched from the door, his expression unchanging and unreadable.

"Mrs. Foster?" the officer prompted.

Elaine cleared her throat to answer. "Yes, we're all right."

"Then have a good night. We'll be in touch in the morning."

Anybody Want to Play WAR?

"Thank you for bringing him back," Elaine said. The officer nodded to her, climbed back into his police cruiser, and left.

II

Elaine threw some eggs into a pan. She scrambled them with a whisk and tossed the whisk across the kitchen counter.

Her movements were sharp. She didn't speak. Richard took a seat at the kitchen table, but he remained quiet.

Elaine banged the pan of eggs onto a stove burner and switched the burner on.

When Bryce started back to his room, Richard spoke. "I think you need to stay right here. We need to talk."

"I want to go to bed," Bryce said. "I'm tired."

This wasn't altogether true. He doubted he could sleep. He wanted to get on the phone and call the hospital about Cheryl, call Tabby, call *someone.*

"No," Richard said, "you'll sit down right here, because this is nowhere near finished."

Elaine snatched a pot from a cabinet, filled it with water, set it on the stove, and ignited another burner beneath it.

"Say what you have to say," Bryce said.

"Do you understand what you've put your mother through?" Richard asked. "Do you?"

"I didn't do it to hurt her."

Richard threw his arms out. "You don't care about anybody but yourself. You already got yourself kicked out of school. Wasn't that enough? No, that wasn't enough. You're determined to destroy your own future and your family. No one cares about you the way your mother does, but you don't even care, do you? You don't give a damn about anybody but yourself!"

In the kitchen, Elaine stood listening but not looking. She instead watched the impromptu nighttime breakfast that had assumed the brunt of her unspoken frustrations.

Tommy B. Smith

"Maybe I was thinking of myself," Bryce said. "But if I should be worrying about my future, I did the right thing in getting out of here. I hate school and I can't stand this place, either."

"You ungrateful little bastard!" Richard exclaimed. "Do you know what the police just told us? Of course you do. You attacked a man with a baseball bat, that's what he told us, and you apparently shacked up with some woman across town. Someone will probably have to go to court over this. I'm not paying for your mistakes. We're going to stay right here until we get every last bit of this worked out, even if it takes all night long. I told you to sit down. You have a lot to answer for."

"I don't have a damned thing to answer to you for," Bryce said.

Richard took a step toward him. Bryce clenched his fists.

"What are you going to do?" Bryce asked. "Hit me? Come on."

Danger flashed in Richard's eyes. Richard was going to take a swing. Bryce almost knew it. He was ready. He would take it and he would give back as good as he got if not better.

But instead, his mother spoke, and the situation entered a stillness.

"Who is she?" Elaine asked.

"Answer her," Richard said. His eyes never deviated from Bryce's.

"Who is who?" Bryce replied.

"The one you were staying with," Elaine said.

"Her name is Tabby."

"Tabby? Tabby who?"

"Why does it matter?"

Elaine scraped scrambled eggs onto a plate. She dropped the pan into the sink.

"I'll find out who she is," Elaine said, moving back to the stove to turn off the burner. She stirred the pot's contents. "And if I need to, I'll press charges. I'll tell you something else,

134

Anybody Want to Play WAR?

Bryce. I thought I raised you better than this. No matter what you might think, you've gotten yourself into more than you can handle this time, and you don't have the answers. You haven't seen anything of this world yet. You're a child!"

She banged a spoon on the pot heating on the stove. "You stay away from that woman from now on. I don't know who she is or what she thinks she's after, but I will not have some whore ruining your life."

"Whore?" Bryce exclaimed, incredulous. "That's it. Fuck this. I'm leaving."

He walked past Richard. Richard grabbed his shoulder. Bryce twisted and shoved him.

"Don't you fucking touch me," Bryce said. "And *you—*" he confronted his mother now— "don't you ever call her that. You don't even know her. She is one of the best friends I ever had, and maybe you can't understand that because you don't know her, or maybe you just don't know me."

Bryce stepped toward the front door. Richard pointed at him and said, "You step out that door, we're calling the police."

"Go ahead," Bryce said. "I'm tired of the threats. Either do something or shut your mouth."

"I will," Richard said.

Bryce walked outside. He reached the end of the driveway when Richard stepped out and declared, "The police have been called."

Bryce stood at the side of the street, silent, as Richard continued to stand at the front door, watching him. The door remained open and light streamed across the carport until finally Richard withdrew into the house and closed the door.

Like so many other times in the past, Bryce wished he had a cigarette.

The anger had returned, burning and powerful in his mind and deep within his chest. He felt like he was suffocating, and he could find no sanctuary, no escape but the fiery path right into an all-consuming blaze.

III

Behind the house, a green tarp covered the lawnmower. Beside this rested a metal gasoline can.

Bryce seized the gas can, walked around the house, and slung gasoline against the house's frame, from its back length around to the left side.

He felt the matchbook at the bottom of his pocket. He brought it out, flipped it open, and struck a match. When it flared, he touched it to the side of the house.

The flame licked the gasoline and became hungrier, stronger, following the splash-trail along the side of the house. The smell of burning wood filled Bryce's senses and the fire rose.

IV

Inside the house, Elaine sat in a kitchen chair with her face in her hands. She raised her tear-streaked, bewildered eyes and asked Richard, "Do you smell smoke?"

Richard opened the front door and stepped outside. Bryce flung the gasoline can past him and ran. It clanged against the wall of the house, bounced against the top of the Pontiac, and tumbled down to the carport.

Elaine saw the fire rising in the kitchen window and sprang to her feet. She ran outside, past Richard, screaming. "Fire! The house is on fire!"

The stench of burning was undeniable as the fire spread. It had erupted across the side of the house and now spread to the back.

Richard ran around to the back of the house, yanked the green tarp from the lawnmower, and hurled it against the house in an effort to stifle the flames. Instead, the fire intensified.

He threw the tarp aside and tried to reach the water hose connected to the back of the house but couldn't get near it for the fire.

He ran to the front of the house, shouting. Elaine stood shocked in the middle of the front lawn until Richard grabbed her, and the two fled from the dancing orange fire that enveloped their home.

V

Sirens blared through the night. A fire truck careened by, red lights spinning and siren howling toward the blaze. Blue lights followed. As two police cars parked along the street, the St. Charles Fire Department hurried to action. Elaine's screams had woken the neighbors. The shouts of the fire department's coordinated efforts brought out more of the residents along Evelyn Drive.

Everyone came outside to see the burning house.

The fire department turned the hose onto the house of Richard and Elaine Foster, battling the raging fire. Elaine sobbed. Richard babbled frantically at the police. One officer hurried to his vehicle and entered a rapid exchange on his radio.

It wasn't long before the police caught Bryce fleeing on foot along Dartmoor Road.

A Place Without Choices

I

Bryce met a lot of angry teenagers in juvenile detention. Some weren't entirely unlike him; they were here because they fought battles within their own homes or schools and had carried the fight outside the boundaries of the law. Some were violent offenders, others thieves. Another was caught selling drugs on the campus of Bryce's own school. As far as Bryce knew, he was the only one here for arson.

Richard had his wish, in a way. Bryce was in a corrective institution, though it wasn't the military school Richard had threatened him with. It was a place with cells, dirty gray-and-green walls, and guards, a place without choices. Over the passing days of solitude in his cell, Bryce had ample time to think.

He often thought about Tabby. He had told his mother Tabby was one of the best friends he ever had, but how could that be true? He had only known her a couple of days. Had it been another lie, or was it just the pathetic truth?

The night he had kissed Tabby, she had told him he had his whole life ahead of him, but where could he go from here? More than ever before, his future appeared beyond his grasp.

Even so, he knew some distant day would bring a parting

of the firestorm. The world was vast, and as it happened, he didn't know much about it. He hadn't seen anything outside of St. Charles.

He kept to himself when he could, his head down most of the time. While other kids fought each other and pushed against the system with every opportunity, Bryce kept thinking to himself, *I just want out.*

During the routines of daily classes and mealtimes, he couldn't always tune out the crowd. It placed him on edge. He remained quiet and pretended to focus on the matter at hand, whether it meant a tray of unappetizing mess that passed for a meal or a droning lecture from a teacher or instructor, but he couldn't shed his tension.

One day during lunch, after the guards herded them into the stone-walled cafeteria again, he noticed some of the other kids at the long table watching him.

When the guards were sparse and out of earshot, one of those kids, the stocky one with short-buzzed hair they called Jimbo, said audibly to the two next to him, "Look at the new guy over there. Ugly as fuck, ain't he? What's wrong with his face?"

When Bryce turned toward them, Jimbo spouted, "What the fuck you looking at?"

Bryce flipped his tray of noodles and red sauce at them. Jimbo flinched and the other two recoiled when the awful food showered over them. Enraged, Jimbo jumped to his feet.

Bryce followed in fast. He lunged across the table with a right hook to Jimbo's head. Jimbo locked his arms around Bryce and slammed him into the floor. Before Bryce could recover, Jimbo and his two lackeys kicked him several times, dazing him, until the guards came in shouting and hauled them away.

The others insisted that Bryce had started the fight. His ribs and back bruised and aching, Bryce spent the remainder of the day alone in his small cell.

Anybody Want to Play WAR?

II

The next day, the guards took Bryce out of his cell with a stern warning. This time, the burly uniformed guards arranged extra distance between him, Jimbo, and the other two kids.

This didn't deter Bryce. The next time he spotted Jimbo in the lunchroom, he set a rapid course toward him.

Before the guards could intervene, Bryce seized Jimbo by the shoulder and punched him in the face. Jimbo wasn't ready this time. He swung an awkward blow and Bryce hardly felt it. He knocked Jimbo to the floor, dropped to pin one of his arms to the floor, drove a knee into his stomach, and hit him over and over until blood covered his knuckles.

The guards screamed in his ears. They dragged Bryce away and slammed him to the floor.

Jimbo moaned from the floor. Blood seeped from his mouth and nose. From nearby, Jimbo's two friends gaped.

The guards tossed Bryce back into his cell. He went without lunch, not that he gave a damn, because the food here was shit.

After that day, most of the other kids gave him his distance.

III

Now there was another kid sitting near Bryce who wouldn't shut up. He was close to the same age as Bryce, and kept complaining about the guards, the food, and every other aspect of their treatment in the facility. He added at the end of his rant, "Just wait till I get out of here. I'll take this shit to court!"

The kid's name was Kurt. He had experienced a few brushes with authority while here, by Bryce's understanding, and most were his own doing.

"The way they treat us in here is bullshit," Kurt said. "Like we got no rights at all and we're not even human. It ain't right, man. They say this is a free country? Shit. My dad took a bullet for this country."

Bryce endured Kurt's complaints in silence. He didn't feel like talking. The odds were that it would lead nowhere and definitely not out of this place.

"Vietnam," Kurt continued, heedless of Bryce's non-participation. "His purple heart's still framed up on the mantle."

Bryce stared at his tray of mystery meat and cabbage. This round of slop was even nastier than yesterday's slimy excuse for spaghetti.

Kurt slumped with his elbows against the lunch table. He fell into a sullen silence of his own.

"My Uncle Jax fought in Vietnam," Bryce said.

Kurt lifted his head and looked over. "He tell you any stories about when he was over there?"

"He never talked about it to me."

"My dad didn't talk it much, either," Kurt said. "He came back and tried to go back to his life like normal, but I could tell something wasn't right. Sometimes he would stare off into space for a long time and wouldn't say anything or answer anybody. He and my mom started accusing each other of random shit and fighting about stupid things. Then one night he jumped out of bed yelling something about 'Charlie' and threw my mom across the bedroom. Gave her a black eye."

It ended there, because the guards were shouting orders at them and the time had come to empty their trays and move out.

IV

The exchange with Kurt was the only real scrap of conversation Bryce had experienced since coming into juvenile detention. Despite mentioning Uncle Jax and the Vietnam War, Bryce couldn't remember the war or the day Jax came home from it, but he remembered those days when he had felt like part of a family, not like now, and he remembered a game from his childhood days on the playground.

A kid clung to the bars of the jungle gym, chanting repeatedly across the playground, "Anybody want to play war?"

The kid looked toward Bryce as he said it. The challenge in his stare reminded Bryce of those three kids who had watched him on the street corner.

Soon after, on that night when Uncle Jax stood outside with his rifle, his silent message clear to everyone on the street, Bryce learned that if someone pushed you, you could push back.

"Anybody want to play war?" the kid repeated.

"I'll play," Bryce said.

Down the hill at the far end of the playground, the other team raced to build their fort of sticks and branches. They didn't count on a surprise attack.

Bryce and the two others on his team charged over the hill, throwing rocks. Bryce aimed for their heads and flung the rocks hard but didn't manage to hit a single one of them.

One of the school's teachers, a sour gray-haired woman named Ms. Hurst, appeared on the hill behind them, yelling. She marched them away for a stern questioning.

"Were you throwing rocks?" Ms. Hurst demanded. "You'd better tell me the truth. The truth will get you farther than anything!"

Like a fool, Bryce admitted he had thrown rocks. The other kids denied their part. The teacher let them go and dragged Bryce to the principal's office for a hefty measure of discipline and a call to his mother.

From then on, Ms. Hurst had watched him, and every slight infraction, even sometimes imagined, ensured another visit to the office. Among the more imaginative accusations were those of his tampering with a water fountain and later dropping his pants to the girls on the playground. Bryce had committed neither of these acts, but Ms. Hurst believed he had, as did the school principal and his own mother in the end.

Disciplinary action became the norm, and "the truth will get you farther than anything" had been a lie.

Bryce didn't share these memories with the therapists. He didn't provide anything more than necessary, even when they asked about his life, his home, his mother, or even his real father, a man who had left before he could remember and of whom his mother never gave a direct explanation.

He knew they didn't care about any of it. They were just doing their jobs.

He answered their questions but kept his answers short. When they asked him about his scar, he told them a dog did it.

They asked him why he set the house on fire. He told them he was angry and found a can of gasoline.

"You do realize we're trying to help you?" asked the man in thick-rimmed glasses from an elevated chair. He delivered the question in a near-monotone.

"Sure," Bryce said with almost as much enthusiasm.

The therapist's attention didn't deviate from his notebook or his scribbling. Bryce imagined he was doodling.

V

Once Bryce became accustomed to the daily routine, one day ran into another, and the days ran into weeks. Because of his encounters with Jimbo, the guards maintained a vigilant watch on him until, after more than a month later, Jimbo disappeared. He had been transferred to another facility, Kurt said.

"Good riddance," Kurt added before returning to one of his favorite topics. "I can't wait till I'm out of this damned place."

"Me too," Bryce said, "but it looks like I'm stuck here."

"Don't sweat it," Kurt said. "We'll get out of here one

day. They can't keep us locked up in here forever."

"Try telling them that."

"I did."

"You ain't going nowhere," another kid, Jerome, said.

"I bet you fifty dollars I get out of here before you do," Kurt countered.

"See, the problem with you is, you don't know when to shut your damned mouth," Jerome said. "That's gonna cause you more problems than anything. Not like Bryce here. He keeps his mouth shut, does what he's told like a good boy. He'll probably get out of here before any of us."

This comment annoyed Bryce. He hadn't been into trouble since that last fight with Jimbo, but he wasn't looking to extend his stay any longer than necessary. He hated this place even more than he had hated his own home and school.

"How about it, man?" Jerome asked Bryce.

"What?" Bryce replied. He prodded the wad of wannabe spaghetti on his tray.

"Why you so quiet?" Jerome asked.

"Because I don't have shit to say," Bryce said. "Now leave me alone."

VI

When his first phone call came, Bryce didn't want to answer it, but the bearded guard who came for him acted as if he didn't have a choice. He gripped Bryce by the shoulder and escorted him through the hallways into an office where another heavyset guard leaned on a desk cluttered with paper, pens and pencils, a radio, and an open bag of potato chips. The guard who had led Bryce here pushed him toward a folding metal chair.

Bryce sat down. One of the guards handed him the phone. He placed it to his ear.

"Bryce?" his mother's voice spoke. "Are you there?"

"I'm here," he said.

"I'm calling to check on you," she said. "I hope you're okay in there. I'm sorry I haven't visited. I—we—thought you needed some time, and to be honest, we needed some time, too. What you did—look, you aren't stable, and you need help, but now you're getting it."

Bryce didn't respond.

"I want the best for you," she said.

"Are you sure about that?" he asked.

"What do you mean?"

"Nothing at all. Thanks."

For a while, his mother remained quiet.

"I'll let you go," she finally said.

Bryce handed the phone to the guards. The guard who had brought him motioned for him to stand and led him back along the hallways to his cell.

Going Nowhere

Between mealtimes, lock-up, therapy, and the classes he and the rest were forced to attend every day, Bryce felt like a rodent treading an endlessly spinning wheel.

"They can't keep us in here forever," Kurt reiterated one day.

Many of the other kids still stayed away from Bryce. Rumors had circulated about him. They said he had stabbed another kid, which wasn't true, but when Jerome asked him about it, Bryce didn't dispute it. Kurt didn't, either.

Less than an hour after lunch, when Bryce sat on the floor of his cell with his back against the wall, the guards came to tell him he had another phone call. He accompanied them to the office, where one of the guards shoved a black telephone into his hand.

"Bryce, this is your mother," Elaine spoke over the telephone. "How are you?"

"It's another day."

"Rhonda asked about you."

"Who's Rhonda?"

"Rhonda, our next-door neighbor. Remember?"

Bryce's eyes strayed up the office's white wall. Yes, he

remembered her, but he couldn't care less. "I sure wish I had a cigarette."

"You shouldn't be smoking," his mother responded.

"Why?"

"You aren't old enough, for one. And it isn't good for you."

"Yeah, well, as soon as I can get a cigarette, I'm having a smoke, I don't care what anybody says."

One of the guards glared at him. The other eyed his watch.

"Don't you want to take care of yourself?" his mother asked. "Why are you *like* this?" Even over the phone, she couldn't hide her exasperation.

"Because I haven't had a cigarette in a long time," Bryce said.

He heard murmuring in the background, his mother and Richard having an exchange. When she returned to the phone, her tone was quiet, almost defeated.

"Okay, Bryce, I'm going to let you go. I'm sorry you're so angry with me. I wish things were different."

"Don't we all?" he replied.

II

"As soon as I get out of here," Kurt said one day at lunch, "I'm going to load up my brother's rifle and shoot a bunch of birds."

"What the hell for?" Jerome asked.

"Because that's what I like to do sometimes. My brother's almost never home, so sometimes I'll get his .22 rifle, go outside, and *boom,* feathers flying, crows coming down. Until my dad runs outside yelling at me to stop. Doesn't usually take too long."

"I'll tell you what I'm doing soon as I get out of here," Jerome said. "I'm gonna get so drunk I can't even stand up!"

"Then what?"

"I don't know, man. Maybe I'll eat a big bag of pretzels or some shit. Who cares?"

"Hey, Bryce," Kurt said.

Bryce jabbed his food with his fork. "What?"

"You got any plans for when you get out of this place?"

"I'm not worrying about it. It looks like I'll be here for a while."

Kurt voiced his mantra again. "They can't keep us in here forever."

"You keep telling yourself that," Bryce said. "But it's up to them, not us."

III

After another month, maybe more, the guards came to tell Bryce he had another call. They took him to the phone. He answered with nonchalance.

"What is it?"

"Bryce? Is that you?"

He recognized her voice, and it wasn't his mother this time.

"Paloma? What the hell?"

"It's good to hear you're still alive," she said.

"How did you find me? And what's been going on?"

"A lot. What about you?"

"They won't tell me anything in this place. I don't even know when I'm getting out of here."

"Keep hanging on."

"I don't know why you're even bothering with me. How is everybody? I haven't heard anything. How's Tabby?"

"Tabby is fine."

Bryce had many questions, but he didn't know where to begin. "Tabby is fine" didn't tell him much of anything.

He settled on asking, "What about Cheryl?"

"She's getting by. She was in a cast for a while. She can walk again now."

"That's good to hear, at least," Bryce said. "How's Wheels?"

"About the same as before, except he has his license back and he's driving again." She paused. "You shouldn't have done what you did with his bicycle."

"So, you know about that," Bryce said. "And I guess Wheels knows, too. I borrowed it and I would have brought it back, but the Sevens came after me—"

"That's enough," Paloma snapped, cutting him off. This startled Bryce. Why did she seem more agitated by the bicycle incident than anything else?

"Take some responsibility," she said. "And stop bullshitting me."

"I'm telling the truth."

"You stole his bicycle. You've been a liar and a thief and treated your friends like shit."

This rendered Bryce speechless. He wasn't angry, just stunned.

"But I'm not calling you to pass judgment, even if I am being fair," Paloma said. "I'm not perfect. I've done things in the past, things I don't talk about. I told you they used to call me Lady Luck, didn't I?"

"Yeah."

"I also told you luck had little to do with my game. When things got desperate, I did what I could to give luck a push into my favor."

"Give luck a push?" Bryce echoed, not quite following.

"To take action as necessary. I didn't always do the noble thing. That's one reason why I haven't given up on you yet, even if you've completely pissed me off. But that's you and me. I can't guarantee others will see it that way."

She stopped. Bryce heard a thudding in the background.

"What's that?" he asked.

"Someone at the door," Paloma said. "I have to go. As I said, keep hanging on. You'll be out eventually."

With a click, the conversation ended.

Anybody Want to Play WAR?

Over the days and months to pass, Bryce's life in juvenile detention meandered into discordant noise much like the roaming blues guitar that characterized the final minute of the last song on Beaumont Smiley's *Broken Road Blues*. Still, Paloma's words resurfaced amid his churning thoughts more than once.

1981

The World Outside

I

Bryce huddled in his rough little cell, lingering on dreams of the world outside these dirty concrete walls. Inside and outside the walls of the juvenile detention facility, time drifted on.

Another year had gone. So had another birthday.

Bryce's mother had come to visit him that day. Tense, timid, and apprehensive, she didn't speak much, but asked him how he was doing, wished him a happy birthday, and left him alone.

Sometime before that, during the fall, Kurt made his exit with, "Man, I can't believe I'm finally getting out of this place."

To Jerome he said, "Looks like you owe me fifty bucks, sucker."

Yet Bryce remained. After Kurt's exit, he wasn't much for conversation with any of the others, not even Jerome.

Apparently looking to repair this lapse, Jerome waited until they were out of the guards' attention one day and prodded Bryce with an unlabeled glass bottle.

"Try some of this," he whispered. Bryce swung a quick glance around the room. The guards weren't looking, and no one else was, either. He took a hit from the bottle and slipped it back to Jerome.

The thick, minty stuff wasn't bad as far as liquor went. It took the edge off. The problem was, it also got Bryce busted. Sort of.

He didn't have a clue of how Jerome managed to smuggle the bottle of peppermint schnapps into the facility and didn't know how the guards found out about it, but they did. When they stomped into his cell later to question him, he denied everything.

"You're a liar, Gallo," one of the guards declared. "We can smell it on your breath!"

"Where did you get it?" the other guard asked. "Tell us the truth or so help me, you'll be in a world of hurt before this is over with."

Bryce told them nothing, and the threat rang hollow, but the next day, Jerome was absent from the lunchroom. Bryce never saw him again.

The guards held a closer eye on Bryce for a while after that, but that incident aside, he hadn't seen much trouble since the fight with Jimbo last year. Within weeks, the guards' attention landed elsewhere.

Bryce fell into the background, not only to the guards, but to everyone in the facility. Most didn't speak to him and often didn't even look at him. He preferred it that way. It was easier to breathe and think.

His therapy sessions became shorter. His therapist was optimistic. Some lies took longer than others to perpetuate. He hoped he had moved a step closer to getting out of here. This place was no better than a crusty hole in the ground.

II

Anybody Want to Play WAR?

Two weeks after his final therapy session, suspicious news arrived. Thinking it might be a sadistic joke at his expense, Bryce didn't believe a word of it until the guards escorted him outside to where his mother stood waiting.

His long-awaited release didn't come with a wave of relief. It came with tension and uncertainty.

They left the building and walked to the car, still the white Pontiac. His mother had managed to tame her hair for the occasion, but her eyes darted toward him a bit too often, and they held a glimpse of fear.

She unlocked the car. They climbed in. His mother fastened her seat belt and started the engine. When she reached down to the gear shift, she hesitated.

Sensing her desire to speak, Bryce waited until she asked, "Could you please put on your seat belt?"

Bryce reached for the strap, pulled it down, and clicked it into place.

Elaine pushed a hand through her dense, curly hair, shot a glance into the rear-view mirror, and shifted the car into reverse. Once backed out, she shifted into first gear and drove through the juvenile detention center's parking lot to the adjoining street to take them home.

Return

I

Richard didn't welcome Bryce home. He remained in the living room, on the edge of the couch, and watched the news in silence.

Elaine tidied up the kitchen and dining area. Bryce walked into his room, closed the door, and sank onto the bed.

Richard made no effort to join Elaine and Bryce at supper. Elaine set a plate aside for him. He reheated it later and ate alone.

Elaine had become noticeably quieter. During the mornings after Richard left for work, she stayed in the living room with a book—on Monday and Tuesday, a copy of *Colour in the Winter Garden* by G.S. Thomas.

Words were few. Warmth was absent.

Bryce shut himself into his room and contemplated the green phone beside his bed. He had thought about Tabby countless times during the days in juvenile hall, but when he placed his hand on the phone, he stalled.

What could he say to her? What would *she* say?

He reached a decision, dialed a number, and waited as the phone rang.

"Hello?" a man's voice answered.

"Hello, is Finn over there?"

"Yeah, hold on."

Finn answered. "Who is it?"

"It's Bryce."

Finn hesitated, but asked, "How's it going?"

"Miserable. You?"

"Okay. I got a car a few months back. It's this big brown thing. My dad calls it the Brown Beast."

"You'll have to show me sometime."

Finn paused. "So you really set your house on fire, huh?"

II

"It can't go on like this, Elaine."

"What do you expect me to do? He's my son."

"Do you understand what he did?" Richard pressed. "What are we supposed to do, pretend it never happened? Pretend we didn't have to rebuild the house over the past year, ignore the way the people on this street look at us, and act like everything's suddenly better and we're some kind of a happy family?"

"Richard." Elaine's voice almost pleaded. "I'm sure he's sorry for what he did."

"Sorry isn't good enough."

That's when Bryce, who had stopped near the bedroom door at overhearing their conversation, opened the door.

"I'm right here," he said. "I can hear every word you're saying."

Richard stood with his white shirt unbuttoned, and Elaine in a blue bathrobe with her hair wrapped in a white towel, both of them staring at him.

"I know what I did," Bryce said. "And you want to know something? I don't feel bad about it."

"Bryce," his mother said. Whatever he meant to say, her wide eyes implored him to stop.

"You've told me plenty of times what I'd better do and

what kind of person I should be," Bryce said to Richard. "You think I should be more like you, but I don't want to be like you. Disappointed? Good. Yeah, you haven't said anything to me lately, and I think that's because we've finally gotten it all out in the open. I don't feel bad about what I did. I feel bad because I got caught, and that's about it."

"How can you say such horrible things?" Elaine blurted.

"Because that's who I am," Bryce said. "You should be happy I'm walking out of here today."

He made one last trip to his room to grab his jacket and slung it over his shoulder on his way out. His mother followed him outside and rushed after him to the driveway.

"What did you mean by all of that?" she asked him, bewildered. "Are you coming back?"

"I'll be fine," he said. "Don't worry about me."

She swallowed and stared at him.

"I'll call Finn," he said. "He'll pick me up. Don't worry."

He started away again, but she said, "Wait."

She came close and pushed something into his hand—a pocketknife, a stainless-steel Sterling.

"This is yours," she said.

He looked it over. "You got it back."

"My brother gave it to you. He would want you to have it."

Then, to his surprise, she slipped a folded wad of dollar bills into his hand, several twenties.

"Happy birthday," she said. "Even though your birthday isn't for another month."

"Does Richard know about this?" Bryce asked.

"I didn't tell him."

"Thanks."

His mother leaned in to hug him. "You're my only son. Please call me when you get where you're going."

She watched him walk to the end of the driveway, where he turned along Evelyn Drive and followed it toward the busier stretch of Dartmoor.

Somewhere in her doubts, among her tears, Bryce supposed she found an odd silver of relief.

The future appeared as it often had to Bryce's eyes, vague and cloudy, but although he walked away today, at least he wasn't running away.

III

Moving along Hatch Street, Bryce passed Tuck's Corner Store. He had a thought of going in but dismissed it as another distraction and continued on. He didn't need anything.

Past the closed-down furniture store, the gift shop, and the florist, he saw the gray apartment building of 2803 Hatch Street.

The apartment building was a bolder gray, darker. Someone, possibly Wheels, had repainted it during Bryce's absence. Bryce hadn't been here in well over a year.

He scanned the cars in the lot, searching for a small brown hatchback, and didn't see one.

Entering the lot, he looked toward the once-empty apartment he had stayed in. He wondered whether anyone lived there now. His eyes fell to the apartment beneath it, the one whose resident he had never seen, and up to the apartment Wheels stayed in—or *had* lived in over a year ago. Bryce didn't know whether Paloma or Wheels were still around.

He had thought a lot about calling Tabby. The notion of calling Paloma had crossed his mind as well, but he wouldn't have known where to start. He didn't even know her last name, but aside from his mother, she was the only one who had called him in juvy, so here he stood, hoping he wouldn't be unwelcome.

At his knock, no one answered. He went upstairs and tried apartment #3. This time, he heard someone fumbling with the door on its other side. It opened and a sallow-faced old man gawked at him.

"Sorry," Bryce muttered.

"Who are you?" the man asked.

"Nobody," Bryce replied, going back down the stairs.

"What do you want?" the man insisted.

He followed Bryce down the stairs. "Hey!" the man shouted. He maintained pursuit, and at the bottom of the stairs, Bryce whirled to face him.

"You'd better back the fuck off right now, old man," Bryce said.

The man fell back against the stairs, his mouth open, aghast.

Bryce resumed his pace across the parking lot back to Hatch Street, where he continued his path along its shoulder.

IV

At the Laundromat, the Asteroids machine had gone dark. A paper sign taped across its screen read *Out of Order* in black marker-scrawl. Unlike the arcade game, the pay phone in the corner remained in perfect working order.

Bryce approached the window where the lone attendant worked, got his change, and dropped a coin into the pay phone. He dialed a number.

"Yeah?"

"Hey, Finn," Bryce said, "you said you have a car now, right? Can you come out and pick me up? I'm at the Laundromat over on Hatch."

"I don't know if I have time. I have to be at work soon. I've been working down at the Spring Market, did I tell you that?"

"You didn't say anything about it. Good for you, though."

"I have to take off in just a few minutes."

"Don't worry about it, then."

"All right, man. I'll catch you later."

Bryce hung up. It occurred to him that he hadn't seen Finn since before the day that dog had attacked him.

Finn hadn't seen the dog's vicious mark on him. He didn't understand why or how Bryce's course had veered so sharply.

Finn had his own future to attend to, besides—and there was absolutely nothing wrong with that.

Bryce reached into his pocket, jingling the change that remained, and deliberated in front of the phone. He knew calling Finn wasn't the real reason he stood here.

He had wanted to call her for so long, but in juvenile detention, he had lacked the freedom to do so. Now it came down to fear—fear of facing the truth of the past, and nothing could stop him but himself.

He lifted the telephone from the receiver, swallowed down a lump of uneasiness, and slid in his coin. No more excuses.

After the operator put him through, the phone rang twice and a female voice, not Tabby's, answered the phone.

"Tabby Reinhart's residence."

"Cheryl? Is Tabby there?"

"Who is this?"

"This is Bryce."

No one spoke for some time, until Cheryl asked, "Don't you think she's been through enough? What makes you think she wants to talk to you now?"

"Maybe she doesn't," Bryce said. "But I thought I should call, give her an explanation, an apology, something."

Silence answered him. He began to wonder if Cheryl had hung up on him, until a rustling sound signified the passing of the phone. A familiar voice spoke at the other end.

"This is Tabby."

"It's good to hear your voice again," Bryce said. "It's been a long time."

"What do you want?"

"I'm sorry about what happened. I'm sorry for everything."

"I don't understand you. Why couldn't you have been honest with me? I would have found out the truth eventually, but finding out the way I did? It was awful. Especially after everything that happened that night. I'll never forget what he did to Cheryl. He could have killed her. I couldn't even be with her in the hospital, not for a while, because the police were questioning me about harboring a runaway minor. You never even told me your real name. How was I supposed to feel about that? I felt like such an idiot."

"I didn't mean to hurt you. Not you, of all people. You were always good to me, even if I didn't deserve it."

Tabby fell silent. When she spoke again, she said, "You were on the news."

"The night of Loveless's attack?"

"Something about you starting a fire. Your own parents' house, wasn't it?"

"That's right."

"Why would you do such a thing?"

"It's complicated." But it wasn't, not really. It was simple.

"I couldn't believe it when I saw it. You're full of little surprises, I'll give you that."

"I probably wouldn't do it again."

"That's a relief." Tabby paused before saying, "I'm not sure what you've heard, but—it hasn't been easy for me." She drew a tentative breath. "Did you hear about George Loveless?"

"Loveless? What about him?"

"He went to jail for a while. After they released him, he went downtown, bought a gun, and shot himself."

Bryce wasn't certain what to say to this.

He noticed a faint quiver in Tabby's voice as she added, "I keep thinking, I'm the one who fired him. If only there had been another way."

"You shouldn't blame yourself," Bryce said. "He's the one who pulled the trigger. It isn't your fault any more than it's mine."

"Well, it's done, and there is nothing anyone can do about it now."

"At least you're safe now," Bryce said. "Or as safe as anybody can be in downtown St. Charles, which isn't much."

"That's why I keep a gun under my sofa cushion. And I still have Cheryl. She takes care of me. We take care of each other." A note of apprehension entered her tone. "Maybe there's something I should tell you."

"About what?"

"Cheryl is my assistant, I told you. She's also a friend. She's also—more than a friend."

"What do you mean?"

"I mean there are certain things I don't tell everyone, but if it's true that you ever were a friend of any kind and you want to prove that to me, you'll respect who I am as a person and not tell anyone what I've just told you."

"Fair enough."

"So now we have the truth between both of us," Tabby said. "What else can we do but learn to live with who we are? I don't want to hide in the dark anymore, and you're still young. As I told you before, you have your whole life ahead of you. I wish you the best, Bryce. I should go. Take care of yourself."

V

Bryce walked along Hatch Street again. Traffic clogged the street, remnants of the evening's rush.

Within an hour, the traffic lessened. The blaring of horns abated. The sun's orange brilliance sank into the horizon. Twilight darkened the city.

He studied the cracks in the edges of the street's blue pavement. A brisk wind flung his hair into disarray. He shoved his hair back and absently touched his face, running his fingers along his scar.

No matter what came his way in the years to come, the mark would never go away, but he was learning to live with it, and with himself, in more ways than one.

Anybody Want to Play WAR?

Light fled the road ahead until the streetlights flickered on. They accomplished little to dispel the darkness of the street, its unlit structures and the black voids between.

Bryce reached into his pocket for the cool reassurance of the stainless-steel pocketknife. He had traveled this way before, but never alone on foot on a night like this.

Paloma

I

Within one establishment among the cluster of Candle Square, Paloma poured a whiskey sour for a patron. She wore a swirly green-and-white loose-fitting dress. A blue sash wrapped her waist. A green wrap secured her dark hair to one side. She wore the turquoise earrings she had worn on the day Bryce met her.

He remembered this as he purchased two packs from the cigarette machine near the front door, shoving one into his pants-pocket and the other into a pocket of his jacket. When he plunged deeper into the dim interior to approach the purple-lit bar, she was quizzical, but not overly startled.

"Of all the bars in all the towns in all the world, you walk into mine," she said.

"I've been out and around. This is where I ended up."

"You're home again now?"

"Home's where the heart is. That's what they say, right?"

"You left?"

"Maybe it's better for everybody."

She placed her hands against the inner edge of the bar and shifted forward. "Have you called Tabby?"

"I talked to her earlier."

"And?"

He didn't give a direct answer, but the slight shake of his head was enough.

"Then you heard about George Loveless," Paloma said.

"Yeah."

"It's been hard for Tabby."

"I told her she shouldn't blame herself."

"He called her, you know."

"Called her?"

"He called her before he did it. They say he went into a pawn shop downtown and hovered around looking at guns for half an hour. He finally picked one out and went out to a phone booth a couple of streets over. Someone saw him standing inside the phone booth for a long time, just holding the phone. Then he called Tabby."

"She didn't say anything about it."

"No, she wouldn't have. She doesn't want to talk about it anymore, but she still thinks about it."

"What did he say to her?"

"She said she had an awful feeling when she answered the phone and recognized his voice on the other end. He asked, 'How does it feel?' She didn't know what to say, and then he said, 'To win. How does it feel? I hope it was all worth it.' He held the gun to his temple, and I'm sure you know the rest."

Bryce swallowed and looked to the dark surface of the bar.

Paloma reached up to take down a short glass. She poured a ginger ale over ice and slid it across the bar to Bryce.

"Don't you have anything stronger?" he asked.

"Not for you," she said. "I don't plan on getting myself fired today. Can you give me a minute?"

A man with gray hair, a rumpled suit, and a loosened burgundy tie had taken a seat at the far end of the bar. Paloma moved to take his drink order. She brought out a frosted glass, into which she drew a golden lager from a tap and delivered it to the waiting customer.

She slipped through a dark opening and emerged to the other side of the bar, near where Bryce stood, but stopped to engage a woman with short, curly dark hair, asking, "Jill, can you cover me? I'm taking my break."

While Jill took over at the bar, Paloma guided Bryce to a square table against the far wall. Bryce carried his ginger ale to the table.

"Are you hungry?" Paloma asked.

"What?"

"I asked if you were hungry. I'll let you in on a little not-so-secret secret: there's a grill in the back. They serve lunch here during the day."

"I don't have any money."

Even in the dimness, Bryce couldn't elude her probing eyes.

He released a sigh. "I do have some money," he admitted. "My mom gave me some for my birthday, but I'm trying to hold onto it."

"It's your birthday?"

"It will be someday. It's still a few weeks away."

"Relax. It's my treat. I'll have Syd throw something on for you."

She left. Bryce slid one of the table's thin chairs back and sat down. He set his glass of ginger ale on the dark table's surface, and soon Paloma returned to sit down across from him.

"So where are you going from here?" she asked.

"That's the question I keep asking myself. I used to talk about getting out of this place. Leaving St. Charles altogether, even though I don't have much money or any idea of where I'm going. Things seem to get worse every day, for me and others."

"There is a darkness in the heart of this city," Paloma mused. "Even as young as you are, you've seen that, haven't you? But many people will cling to this place until they die.

We all have our own choices to make."

An aroma of sizzling meat reached Bryce's senses, and he realized his hunger. He hadn't eaten much today.

When the quiet lingered, Paloma glanced toward a purple-outlined round wall clock. Appearing satisfied, she withdrew a deck of playing cards and commenced shuffling.

Though she remained intent on the cards, Bryce asked her, "So how is Wheels these days? I tried knocking on his door earlier today. Yours too. Instead I met some crazy old man."

"Wheels moved out months ago," Paloma said. "He doesn't work for Tabby anymore. He's a groundskeeper over at Summerset Park. I see him every now and again. He'll come into Pep's for a drink and say hello. He seems content. I told you he was driving again."

"Can you give this to him the next time you see him?" Bryce laid a wrinkled twenty-dollar bill on the table. "For the bike. Wheels told me one time he got it for twenty dollars. That's a good price." After a pause, he withdrew the pack of cigarettes from his jacket pocket and placed it on top of the twenty.

"This too. He'll understand. It isn't much, but it's something."

With a thoughtful nod, Paloma returned to shuffling, quiet for another moment before raising her eyes to Bryce. "Are you up for a game?"

"Against you? I wouldn't stand a chance."

"Oh, I don't know about that. You know the rules, don't you? We'll keep it simple. Seven card stud or five card draw?"

"Blackjack."

"Don't be difficult. Here."

She dealt the cards. Five card draw it was. He picked up his hand, a lot of nothing, and traded three cards for little better, a ten high. Paloma took the game with a queen high.

"I told you," Bryce said, "I don't stand a chance, Lady Luck."

Anybody Want to Play WAR?

Paloma flipped her card, the queen of spades, toward him. "You call that luck?"

"I call it a win, for you."

"Barely, and how much does it matter? We aren't playing for money." She gathered her cards and turned another look at the clock. "It's almost that time. I should get back to the bar."

Paloma swept the cards together, returned them to their case, and stood. She took the twenty and the pack of cigarettes as she left, heading wide of the bar and around a dark corner.

She returned to the table to set a white plate with a sizzling sirloin steak in front of Bryce. "Happy early birthday," she said.

"Thanks," he said.

She leaned over, put her arms around him, and squeezed him. "Enjoy. I have to get back to work."

II

The steak was fresh from the grill, savory and tender with a hint of smokiness, along with a touch of onion.

Once he finished, only a smudge remained on the plate. The other woman from the bar, Jill, showed up to retrieve it with a quick smile.

He dug the other pack of cigarettes from his jeans-pocket. He opened the pack, took out a cigarette, and started to light it but realized he had nothing to light it with.

"Damn," he muttered.

Jill happened by again and saw his empty glass. "Want another one?" she asked.

"Sure," he said.

"What did you have?"

"Jim Beam on the rocks," he lied. "And do you have a light?"

She withdrew a small red plastic lighter, struck it aflame,

and lit up his cigarette. He nodded his thanks, and she went on.

She reappeared a couple of minutes later to set down the glass of whiskey. He handed her a few folded dollars.

Too easy, he thought. He half-expected Paloma to show up and snatch his drink away, but when she didn't, he leaned back to drink the whiskey and smoke his cigarette.

He wasn't used to the whiskey, but that didn't stop him. When the cigarette burned down toward its finish, he snubbed it into the table's round glass ashtray. He finished the last sip of whiskey from the glass of melting ice, pushed it away, and stood up.

He didn't stay much longer, only long enough to approach the bar's purple glow once more and say goodbye to Lady Luck before he returned to the open street that wound deep through the shadowed heart of the city.

About the Author

Tommy B. Smith is a writer of dark fiction, author of The Mourner's Cradle, Poisonous, and the short story collection Pieces of Chaos, as well as works appearing in numerous magazines and anthologies throughout the years. His presence currently infests Fort Smith, Arkansas, where he resides with his wife and cats.

More information can be found on his website at:
http://www.tommybsmith.com

www.ingramcontent.com/pod-product-compliance
Lightning Source LLC
Chambersburg PA
CBHW031454260626
47154CB00017B/2738